NOIR

A novel

Donat ion
CL

NOIR

A novel

KEN CHAMPION

First published October 2016

ISBN 978-1-326-78146-0

Cover photo courtesy Charles Carruthers

PENNILESS PRESS PUBLICATIONS
Website :www.pennilesspress.co.uk/books

For
Toby, Tim, Steve

Urban Narratives

'I thank him for gracing our magazine with his literature. His realism is enriched with imagination, the most real of all qualities.'

Meredith Sue Willis, Hamilton Stone Review USA (2014)

The Beat Years

'I found some beautiful writing here.'

Susie Reynolds, Chimera (2015)

'In his latest novella, Champion returns to the aftermath of war in the grim, treeless, rubble-strewn terraced streets of a still mono-cultural east London.

It sheds light on a long-lost world of black and white television, rigidly defined gender roles and, most importantly, the suffocating straitjacket of class, from the forelock-tugging fawning sycophancy of Ben's father ('a man of few skills his instinct told him that to survive he would have to defer') through to the codes that differentiate the 'respectable' from the 'rough' working class and in the seemingly irreconcilable divisions between classes.

Though informed by these timeless, even epic themes, Champion's descriptive strength comes from his exquisite minituarism and his ability to capture the intimate detail of routine domestic settings. His characterisation is pretty faultless too, like Brilliantined bad boy, Vinny Duggan, frustrated crimper turned greasy-spoon owner, Lou, and there's a lovely cameo of a narcissistic gym master that's worth the cover price in its own right.

Champion's stark and sometimes disturbing stories, told often with anger and a dust-dry wit, manage to reach out to the general reader whilst also generating plaudits from critics and peers. And he is not only prolific, he is near as dammit pitch-perfect as he turns in yet another assured narrative that effortlessly snares the reader and draws us into its grainy, lost world.'

Chris Connelley, Hastings Independent (2015)

CHAPTER 1

He wasn't sure why he was thinking of his former wife - he rarely did - as he parked at the edge of a field with a circus-large marquee, American army jeeps, and men in khaki serge uniforms lining up to take turns bayoneting a sandbag. It was the image of himself standing next to her in the church looking down at her narrow white face, pale eyes, slightly crooked nose and the wedge of out-of-focus people behind them and detachedly seeing himself, almost hearing himself, silently screaming and doing nothing about it, just remaining there, locked into the unreality of it, the denial of it.

Then a quick time-lapse re-run of sleeping in a separate room and the endless escaping: painting a painfully detailed Japanese mural on the through-lounge wall, building a pond, fountain, waterfall and rockery in the garden, often till one at night; the former he was skilled at, had been for a short while a commercial artist, the latter he'd made himself do, though not being quite certain why.

He thought knew why he was here at this World War 2 themed event in Essex, though; it was because of the films he'd seen from an infant onwards and his father's tales of the London Blitz when he'd been a child. It was the former that had the most impact on him: movies like 'Battle Cry,' the more English sounding 'Above Us The Waves' and the almost biblically entitled 'The Sea Shall Not Have Them,' appealing to the Edwardian cultural residue of the time.

After pausing to look in at some of the memorabilia-filled tents around the field's perimeter, he walked towards the marquee as a man dressed in a British Army captain's uniform stood at a stall in front of it and said through his mike, 'Listen up guys,' and announced there would be some jitterbugging going on behind him presently and that anyone could join in. It was the 'guys' that jarred, he was supposed to be an English officer not a Yank - noticing as he thought it, the 'Yank' was a direct internalization from his father, the predictable 'They're oversexed, overpaid, overfed and over 'ere,' and the riposte of, 'You're undersexed, underpaid, underfed and under Eisenhower.' A man dressed in American GI uniform said in passing, ''ello mate,' making him immediately wish that he'd been on the committee organising the event where he would have insisted on cast members' accents being as appropriate as their clothing.

He must have shown a slight annoyance a second before the hint of a smile and the narrowed green eyes of a passing Land Army girl suggested a mild accusation of pedantry. He smiled back at her and watched her walk off, tall and slim, headscarf knot high on her forehead like a war poster, perfectly in keeping with the period as was her khaki shirt and the white apron hiding blue dungarees.

He spotted a burger tent and made for it, trying to breathe away the dryness of a paper he'd just finished for the London Journal of Sociology. He'd felt a little stifled, couldn't seem to lift what he was writing, it was academically hemmed in, he was too used to the obviousness of it, the tired words and, though he'd been asked to do it, had forced himself to. 'Mature students: better at coursework than exams.' wasn't really something that had set his cerebral neurons flowing. Perhaps this visit, which he'd seen advertised in a café, would stimulate something, even if it was only some sort of quasi-nostalgia.

He saw two women, hair and scarf the same as the land girl, but with shoulder-padded frocks and clutched handbags. They were immediately aunt Elsie and her sister Daisy again, bending down, hand cupping his infant chin. 'Who's a pretty boy then?' He was sure that this was what they wore, the style, the material; perhaps they had a thing about their mother's past, her clothes, they'd dressed up in them as kids in the street, maybe dancing, one of them taking the man's part and holding the other firmly around the waist, bending her backwards till her hair touched the pavement.

He watched them walk into the big tent, hastily finished his food and followed them in. He looked again at their wedged shoes, earrings, modest length of frocks and then outside to the soldiers, now finished attacking sandbags, forming a protective line in front of the entrance, each a few feet from where the guy ropes were staked.

They were standing to attention, behind them, crossing the field, were some American servicemen laughing with their girls, their floozies. He resisted going out to ask them if they'd 'Got any gum chum?' and sat at a large table on his own with a menu for 'wartime food' in front of him: rabbit and beef pot - which he suspected was merely meat paste - vegetables, rhubarb tart and custard, but no chicory essence which had passed for coffee in those days.

Other people sat near him as more came into the tent, the servicemen congregating around tables at the far end; these were, he guessed, arrivals for the evening show. A man wearing a naval officer's uniform came onto the makeshift stage at the back and announced in a provincial accent which retained a smattering of fast-dying Home Counties RP that before the food would be dancing.

The sound of boogie-woogie filled the tent and the end tables emptied as their occupants began jiving in front of the stage, most well-versed enough to suggest they went around the county doing the same thing at similar events. Looking around him, he noted that no one was wearing slacks - he remembered his grandmother and sometimes his mother wearing them - nor were there women with a pencilled line down their calves to emulate real stockings, and not a trace of a kipper tie spiv.

The meal was served and after it some Andrew Sisters lookalikes came on stage and sang to 'Boogie-woogie Bugle Boy,' 'Rum and Coca Cola,' and other of the trio's numbers. As he watched them they confirmed the answer to his genesis question, it was Hollywood again, and he let it run though him, wash over him while he clipped his fingers and drummed the table.

He glanced around as if wanting to see someone enjoying it as much as him and saw a figure behind him leaning against a stanchion and wearing a kind of trilby with a net veil covering her face, allowing her dark red mouth prominence. She was very still, gazing steadily across at the singers. He watched her, almost staring, before her eyes moved towards his, holding them for a second before gazing back to the stage. It was the Land Army girl, revamped and dressed like his aunts. He thought he saw through the veil a hint of a smile.

There was a hiatus between the songs, the finishing of the jiving and the sounds of a jeep revving from outside which was ended by a man at his table turning to listeners either side of him with, 'Well, I mean, you know, I mean, what you could say is, you know, they... ' which Vincent, disliking the currently fashionable gushing inarticulacy, internally recoiled from; he was also a little annoyed when the man utilised his mobile as if he, too, was purposely not sticking to the period.

Another announcement, this time asking people who had put money in the memorial fund box to guess heads or tails when the announcer spun a coin by putting their hands on their head or placing them on top of their buttocks. Vincent stood, disinterestedly, almost as a reflex, resting the back of his hands behind him and for four consecutive spins tails came up. The three left standing were invited onto the stage where he placed his hands on his head, guessing the final spin correctly, and was handed a bottle of champagne.

He took it back to his table and wondered if convention held that he should share it with the others sitting around it, but as they were getting up to dance after a final rendering of 'Bugle Boy' he put it down in front of him. He looked over his shoulder. She was still there. She put a thumb up and smiled. He nodded to her and as he made himself look away again heard her say quietly, 'You look like Al Pacino.'

He turned to her again. 'You're not the first to say it and I don't know whether it's flattering, but thanks.'

She smiled once more. 'Pleasure.'

It was the fourth time in as many months he'd been likened to the man. The last time had been when walking out of the loo in a pub outside Euston station and the speaker saying to his friend, ''ere George, look, fuckin' Pacino.' It could have been worse; it could have been Colonel Gaddafi as someone recently said he resembled. He had also been seen as both Italian and Jewish. A week previously he'd been walking through Broadway Market when a man selling curtain material from a stall asked him what shul he belonged to. He'd told him he wasn't Jewish.

'Of course you are; what shul?'

Either would do, both seeming a little more exotic than 'English.' In his youth it had been Dirk Bogarde and, from older family members, Tyrone Power. But he didn't care who he looked like, there were over seven billion people in the world, somebody had to look like somebody.

He wanted to tell her that she reminded him of all the forties actresses he'd ever seen, but diluted it to 'And you're a cross between Jane Greer and, I dunno, Gene Tierney,' even then doubting whether she'd pick up the references, she was younger than him.

'Thank you, I'd have marginally preferred Vivien Leigh, but they'll do.'

She held his gaze; he wasn't sure what to say.

'Er, d'you want to share this bottle with me? I'll get a glass.'

'Thanks anyway. It's kind, but I need to go. Enjoy the rest of the evening.'

She moved casually out of the tent's exit and went away into the beginning of the dusk. He wanted to follow her out, to ask her... what? Maybe where she lived, her phone number, email address, but he didn't, knowing as he turned toward the stage again that he'd regret not doing so. He disliked the instant recognition that this was so much him, doing nothing, inaction.

There was little happening in the tent; the entertainment andfood seemed to have finished, even the announcements, except for one involving the auction of a George Medal belonging to a grey-haired, stooping veteran led to the stage amid applause. He listened to the starting bids then left, looking around him as soon as he was outside to see whether he could see her. A couple came out of the tent, he in shiny dark brown leather jacket, fawn trousers and a flying officer's cap, she in a belted beige frock with a flower over its top button. As they passed him he suggested jokingly to the man that he probably didn't take his outfit off when he got home.

'I don't,' he said, grinning, 'neither does she; we walk about like this most of the time. We go quite a way to get the right stuff.'

They went off, leaving the little boy in him wishing they'd take him home and adopt him. He laughed at himself, walked to his car and drove home.

He went inside; a bit of Art Deco here and there: a stepped lamp - he imagining its translucent blue being a lit tower above a star-studded Chicago night with theatres, ballrooms and Lempicka murals - a couple of Bakelite photo frames, a Clarice Cliff teapot, but no figured walnut or triple mirror; he couldn't afford these things anyway. It all looked so half-hearted. He felt as nondescript as his nondescript East London street.

Next day he went into the city and onto a crowded station concourse and as somebody came towards him looking trancelike down at their phone he stood rigidly so the man bounced off him; another socially atomised individual lost in a solipsistic bubble of phone technology seducing him deeper into a false consciousness.

He thought of the fictional phone he'd created which he called a 'SOMO PZSB: Scared Of Missing Out Phone Zombie's Security Blanket.' The notion that the smart phone and social media was somehow transformative and liberating was incorrect; it was really a perfection of the free market's infiltration of every aspect of people's waking life, its commitment to privatise everything that is public and commercialise everything that's private. His own was more of a dumb phone, like a small brick, but it was all he needed.

Hoping to find some rare public articulacy and a suspension of value judgements, he'd been on his way to a lecture in Tavistock Square given by an apparently 'well known' philosopher and had left after a short while in annoyance at her unawareness of how superficial and mistaken she was in talking of 'young people of this generation' with the inherent implication that working class youths had more in common with their middle class counterparts than with their parents, not understanding that parental cultural values largely determined whether they would or would not go to university and would or would not become manual workers.

CHAPTER ONE

She was, with her vulgarized inductive non-thinking, yet another example of the projection of a privileged life experience onto the rest of the social world. His sensitivity to this often increased when in the company of carriers of such entrenched privilege.

He was, technically, now one of them, but stubbornly wouldn't admit it, preferring instead the concept of *declasse*. It was their liberalism that bothered him. Who was it said, 'scratch a liberal and you'll find a fascist'? He'd even heard someone recently say that it was inexcusable to mention somebody being 'black', and didn't a football club chairman get fined recently for talking of an oriental as a 'slit eye'? Okay, so it could have been derogatory, but he wondered if the liberal elders of Detroit would remonstrate against their black brethren calling a white man a 'honkey,' or Chinese mandarins in Beijing strictly forbidding their countrymen from referring to a white person as a 'round eye.'

He took a deep breath. He had to stop this scornful cynicism. But sometimes it seemed to overtake him. He was aware, at least on a detached level, of his intolerance, but sooner that than mask it all with a suffocating blandness. He began wondering if he was taking it into his teaching. He was lecturing at a local college and had created a course that helped mature students get into higher education - sooner this self-identifying relationship with them than with more educationally endowed students at a university, the latter would be younger, too, and he occasionally had images of himself explaining the definitions and appropriate uses of 'like,' a word which seemed to punctuate their vernacular at least twice a sentence.

The mature students he taught generally had problems, especially women. The majority on his course were females and half of them were starting the long road to economic independence and, for some, hoped-for single parenthood. Their male partners were largely unsupportive, insecure and suspicious of those who were helping their women stretch to new vistas; a colleague had recently seen one of them standing in the car park looking grimly up at the staff room windows for most of a morning. Fresh bruises seemed a weekly occurrence. The younger girls, minimum age twenty, weren't exceptions. He taught a hundred and fifty students split into groups called 'cohorts' by management and had told the latter that as a cohort referred to a tenth of a Roman Legion and he hadn't seen a toga or a sandal since he'd been there, the term was inappropriate.

He disliked management and their sycophants; their eager grabbing of 'edu-biz' buzz words and throwing them into the air like linguistic status symbols at staff meetings, at the end of which, having remained silent throughout, he would quietly place a scribbled list of code words in front of the frowning Chair. The students he saw as 'his,' as he did the subject he taught, and was aware that this proprietary urge was a vestige of a working class background; his father, a caretaker, owning nothing, would claim psychological ownership of 'his' building, his mother, a cleaner, 'her' bank.

Returning home he made himself cook a meal; like gardening, cooking often seemed elevated into an art form by non-artistic people who wanted to kid themselves they were creative. He felt restless and continued reading a recent book on how the immigrant Jews who had invented Hollywood a hundred years ago had, in their eagerness to be assimilated into American life, extolled and exaggerated its values to such an extent that the images they created of the nation, its symbols and the perceptions of them, were entrenched in the world's psyche even to this day. What a good question to set for next term: 'What would capitalism be like without the camera?' Thinking of Hollywood, he saw the big tent again, the clothes, the 'soldiers,' and the girl. He went to bed.

A few days later, a Saturday, he drove vaguely east. It was hot, his neck seemed to be melting; the lower parts of his lungs taking in air as if an afterthought. He wound the windows down and moved faster. Fancying a stopover at a decent café or country pub somewhere, he came off the motorway, saw a 'London 50 miles' sign and realised he'd come further than he thought.

He drove on, the area seeming familiar. The café he stopped outside certainly was, it was the one he'd breakfasted in on his way to Egan Village for the war memorial event. He remembered it mostly for its tea with milk separate, flowers on tables, low, easy listening music, a copy or two of 'Essex Life' and, pleasingly, an old edition of 'The Socialist Worker.' He was remembered; perhaps because he tended to talk to cafe staff, especially in the many cafes he visited in London.

Sometimes he tried to imagine their previous lives. Perhaps the waitress who had his attention here used to twirl *en pointe* around tables in *Cafe Bleu* placing a cup, a croissant mid-step, maybe the girl, plate-stacked in Paulo's and curtsying the kitchen door, had once dropped fries and sunny side eggs in front of a cop on 2nd and Main, and the one he'd seen yesterday had eaten a horse hoof in Chechnya to stay alive, or fled a looted Kabul window and bloodied apron. Sometimes he saw them as legions of mothers offering surrogate suckling. He watched the boss at the entrance twisting his shoe on a fag end then concentrated on his baguette and salad.

He hadn't looked around the village when he was last here; maybe he would now, a departure from his walks around London and its Victorian terraces, Edwardian mansions, its parks and alleys, its bits of architectural magic. He looked out the window and thought he recognised, across the way, the field the event had occupied. It was empty, no stalls, no parking area, no tent, just hedges, tress and grass, almost as if it hadn't taken place.

It was another few days till the end of term then nine weeks off until the new academic year. He needed a project; he'd had them for the last few years. Two summers ago he'd spent veering away from his usual detailed paintings and sketches of buildings and landscapes, mostly the former, to do some abstract stuff. Some he'd put into a gallery but they hadn't sold. The previous summer he'd gone to Barcelona with a friend and looked around the Camp Nou, the Sagrada and sketched the statues on the Ramblas.

As he looked out the window, a man wearing wellington boots came across the field, along the lane a few yards and into the café. He was sweating.

'Good job it weren't loike this larst weekend; all them wartime clothes 'd 'ave bin a bit much, they'd have 'ad to wear them bikinis.' he said to no one in particular as he sat down at the next table.

'I think it was mostly a one-piece then, wasn't it?' asked Vincent.

19

'Dunno, if you say so. Did you go to it?'

'Yes, it was pretty good.'

'You can see why the girls went for the Yanks at the toime carn't yer, them uniforms an' all. Dressed up a bit city-loike weren't they, the girls, 'ceptin' one, she was a land army one. My old grandpa used those in the war, right 'ere on this land, bet 'e got up to some 'anky panky with 'em' He smiled. 'He 'ated those Americans though. There was a lot of 'em this way 'cos o' the airfield. Suppose you couldn't blame the locals, really.'

While he was explaining why, his listener was thinking of barns, corn, cows, dark-haired land girls - he couldn't imagine fair-haired ones now - lying on hay bales or climbing up ladders leaning against ricks, pitchforks in hand, all wearing cork-wedged shoes.

'Bit too neat and toidy for a real land girl though, remember seein' 'em as a boy, mud and shit down their fronts, workin' all 'ours some of 'em, exploited too I 'spect. Apparently there were eighty thousand of 'em all told.'

The farmer's meal came and he began to eat.

Whenever Vincent heard the word 'exploited' he invariably saw himself teaching The Theory of Surplus Value and asking a class, 'Supposing you did work you liked for a bloke you liked; if you didn't feel exploited *would* you be?' Perhaps he should stop asking it, this was an internalized reality of what it felt like, not Marx's constructed one, though it could be argued the former blinded the individual to what actually was. He could feel the start of another fractious, but rather deadening internal battle, they were becoming almost ritualised.

'o' course,' continued the man, cheeks bulging, 'she'd have looked good even if she were covered in muck. She were a looker.'

He pictured her sitting at the side of a domestic ungulate releasing its teats for a moment to brush her forehead, leaving a smear of slime on it then dutifully returning to her task, though it could be she'd never been near a cow, or a farm for that matter. He asked if he knew her, if she was a local girl.

'No, she seemed to be on her own, she's a townie I reckon.'

He thought of the tent again, its height, space, like a fabric aircraft hangar, the grass floor, the tables, uniforms, he wondered why it was so clear, almost a total recall: the girls singing on the stage, the white-starred jeeps, cropped hair of the American 'major' leaning back on a Cadillac, rogering the rear of a Havana with a match before lighting it, and the girl.

'Yeh, loike I say, you can see why the gals went for the G.I's carn't yer.' said the man.

Vincent pictured her being offered some stockings by a white-toothed soldier, she wide-eyed and laughing, and felt a flash of adolescent jealousy. He drank his coffee, bid the owner and his farming customer good day and left, feeling he didn't quite have the energy to walk around in the parched air. He sat in his car for a while before driving home.

He was in an artisan bakery-cum-café that used to be 'Halal Kebab' and looking out at hip-hop teens loping along in jeans with knee-length crotches and shoulders yawing as if they were auditioning for Richard The Third. Around the church opposite, Sunday best Africans coiled like a Technicolor snake while over the road in 'Bindira Sarees' were silks that spoke of duty, wife and mosque, where a girl lifted gauzy cottons the colours of her moods, had perhaps ridden bikes in one and played peek-a-boo in others. Going out to the East End heat he saw acronym fruit, *guava, eddos, saag* on pavement stalls, look-alike heroes on Bollywood posters and girls in salwar kameez playing hopscotch as a posse of 'Wha cha' 'bout mun innit' young Asians slouched by.

He'd wanted a bit of urban grot, pieces of childhood memories and Petticoat Lane, and had sat here trying to relax by looking out at the Edwardian houses across the road. The last time he'd come this way, by a detour on the DLR, he'd asked the female captain, now a bland personnel service assistant, what part of America she was from. She wasn't, instead originating in The Lebanon but being taught by Americans.

He had begun his diatribe on the far-reaching linguistic imperialism of the US with their 'I was like, wow!' and that

Tesco of adjectives, 'awesome,' and that one day instead of referring to American-English it would have become merely 'American,' then stopped. Not wanting to listen to this particular 'The world is American' speech, the driver had given him a false smile then did things with knobs and keys to maintain the smooth functioning of her train.

He glanced at the posters on the wall, most of them advertising films, theatres, pop-up activities and concerts at various venues, and saw that an event marking the 75th anniversary of the London Blitz was on that night. He knew a little about the time, his father having told him of his dad and an uncle digging the back garden and putting a shelter in, the ack-ack guns in the park at the top of the street, incendiaries, doodlebugs, V-2s, neighbours chatting over a twisted garden fence with half their houses gone, and others who'd left most of their belongings with a family in the next street finding, when housed again, that these people had scarpered with them. He was going nowhere special and decided to go, killing a couple of hours beforehand walking around an Arts and Crafts estate nearby of too-small houses and too many scrolls.

It was an old working men's club. He walked up the front steps under the Victorian arch, through the scuffed double doors and into a hall with a bar, bunting, dark wood dado, cream-painted walls and a portrait of King George V1 and his elder daughter. There were about eighty or so people sitting at tables and at the end of the hall a stage with ribbons of gold tinsel and the inevitable half-drunk pint of beer placed on the edge of it.

The octogenarian band, after a short silence as they ended their warm-up, launched into a swing number and, just like before, several American 'GIs' began jiving with their long-frocked, shoulder-padded gals in front of the stage. He watched them for a while, unsure whether they were the same lot that had appeared at the village, then looked about for a table.

She was standing there; that statuesque quality again, no hat or veil this time but a floral pattern frock, hair in waves and those deep red lips. She could have been in a bar off Mulholland Drive, but she also prompted thoughts of his late mother dressing up for one of her rare journeys outside the house: the powder puff, lipstick, the brief tissue between her lips and the quick pulling down of her dress in front of the wardrobe mirror. The image held a comforting pleasure. He looked at her for a while before she turned to him and quietly smiled. He made his way around the tables towards her

'Hello, I saw you at the war memorial do in that village; you morphed from land girl into - '

'A crush from a past fantasy?'

'What are you doing here?'

She frowned. 'Well, 'I'd never been to a themed thing before till the one you saw me at and I met this man who goes around to these places dressed in this period stuff, apparently quite a few people do, and he asked me if I fancied coming and if I could sing or dance. I told him I could do both at a push.'

'Glad you didn't say 'guy,' which incidentally has become a generic term for groups of both sexes, therefore sexist in that - '

'Are you always like this?'

'I'll try not to be.'

The band leader came on stage complete with suit and bow tie and introduced his band and the first quickstep, 'Twelfth Street Rag.' Vincent asked her to dance.

She looked him up and down. 'Only if you dress appropriately: shiny shoes, double-breasted suit and your trilby safely in the cloakroom.'

'Wish I'd hired something, if I'd known you'd be here I would have.'

'Honest?'

'I think so.'

She looked around her. 'You know, I thought that people who dressed up or re-enacted things like the Battle of Hastings or something were rather obsessive nerds, but somehow this feels different.'

'Because you like doing it?'

'Exactly, I've always liked these styles and I heard this thing was on at that village and found a dress, hat and shoes in a charity shop so put them on and went, I enjoyed it.'

For a second he didn't want her to say that, it was too pragmatic, prosaic, he wanted her to be *of* the forties, the mystique of a diffident Englishness, top button of a dress done up, the modest length of leg showing, yet the shiny hair and lipstick a kind of contradiction, like in noir films where men would move downhill through a forest and jump onto rocks across a stream still wearing their fedoras, ties, and raincoats with collars pulled up.

Feeling that the English teacher at the Tech who'd taught the lads ballroom long after it had died would smile proudly, he took a deep breath and led her to a corner near the other dancers and with a gentle pressure on the small of her back smoothed them along, reverse twist here, a spin there, she looking rather uncomfortable. He tried a joke.

'This nun's driving along and clips someone's wing mirror. She stops, walks towards the other vehicle to apologise, when the driver gets out, strides up to her and punches her in the face. As she lies on her back in the road he stands astride her, looks down and says 'Not so clever now are you, Batman.''

She threw her head back and laughed. They danced silently for a minute or so longer, he realising how long it had been since he'd done this, or even held a woman. Since his ex there'd been a few, almost inevitably mature students, though he had never approached them, the reverse being true.

There was Mercia, who used to sit in class, braided extensions rising above a headband, gazing at him with Bambi eyes and a knowing mouth and occasionally sipping brandy from a plastic bottle. He'd thought it was mineral water. It had been a frenetic time: he'd been to a gym with her, seen the frown under the dark nest of hair to ward off posing machos; watched her puffing out her pain in press-ups, drowning her sadness in saunas. He'd held her up in a nightclub, rushed to her bedside in a local hospital because she'd collapsed, gazed at the zigzagging, merging colours on the screen while her liver was being scanned and, after being dragged for a sunset ride on the 'Barracuda' at Southend, lying next to her on his bed like a zombie.

'Excuse me; may I take this lady away from you?'

It was the band leader. He turned to her.

'Billy said you may like to sing something, am I right?'

She was hesitant. 'I can sing a bit; don't know whether I know many of the old ones, though.'

'Shall I leave you to think about it?'

'Erm, 'Bye bye Black Bird,' I suppose.'

'That'll do. Ready now? I'll tell the band. Your name is?'

'Gail.' She looked at Vincent, raising her eyebrows.

The man returned to the stage, announced that he had a volunteer for a song, bent and held his hand out to her which she took and climbed the steps at the side of the stage. A bass strummed; the sound of brushes on a drum then a clarinet took up the tune and, guessing it would be a slow, bluesy version, she began.

'Pack up all my care and woe, Here I go, Singing low, Bye bye blackbird. Where somebody... '

As she sang her confidence seemed to grow, the stiffness easing from her. Holding the hand mike more loosely she began swaying slightly. He didn't know much about singing, but as she sang he wanted to be the somebody that 'waits for me,' and when she reached, 'Make my bed and light the light,' he wished to do those things for her.

When she finished, people clapped enthusiastically, she bowed her head a little, smiled, walked across to the steps, down again and rejoined him.

'I thought you could only sing 'a bit.''

'Well, I happened to remember that one, but I haven't sung since school choir really.'

'Perhaps you should do it more often. Look, let's have a coffee or something.'

He smiled at himself. 'I can't resist saying this, but like countless other men at this moment I'm playing a kind of 'hide the id' game. Almost unconsciously my ego needs to satisfy the demands of the libido but, aware of the constraints imposed by the super-ego, suggests the compromise of meeting in the socially approved environment of a bar or coffee shop.'

'Unconsciously?' she smiled. 'I do need to eat now anyway.'

'There's a buffet here, but let's go outside, find somewhere.'

There was a Turkish place almost next door to the hall, where they ordered identical meals.

'The bandleader will probably come running in soon and ask you to sing the finale or go to Glasgow with him next week to do the same song.'

He looked at the food, the meze, olives and sour bread then at her opposite him. He liked the way she held her cutlery, neatly, tidily, the cutting and picking up silently and ergonomically maximised. He rarely wanted to see people eating, especially holding their forks as if they had arthritic hands, he felt it was a private process, not a public one, knowing, as with many things, where this aversion came from; inevitably childhood and being forced to sit at the table with his parents and trying not to watch his father scraping the remains of a meal and sliding them into his mouth on the end of his knife.

Then an image which hadn't filled his head for years: the smell of sauce on hot chips, inimical, attacking, the memory of dad's fists, the slit eyes, brown teeth, hands smashing down, fork spinning from a plate and arcing into the backroom wall. He shook it from him but not before seeing him outside a pub with vinegar'd cockles, canines ripping a whelk and flexing his calves as if ordering another pint. He looked past her auburn hair at the pavement trees, seeming almost to drip ketchup.

As they ordered baklava he asked her where she lived.

'Mersea.'

'It's a little island place in Essex isn't it?'

'It's an island in an estuary which has been occupied since Roman times and is divided into two main areas which are linked by a causeway which floods at full tide.'

'Why there?'

'Why not?' The house was left to me when my mother died. I like it.'

He listened to her without really hearing; just looked at her, the way she tossed her hair with its shallow waves spreading out, and that grin stretching her lips.

She looked at her watch. 'I need to go.'

'No drink then.'

'No time.'

She stood and took a handbag off the back of her chair.

'Thanks for the meal, though a rather out-of-character one considering the period my clothes represent.'

He offered to walk to the station or bus stop with her.

'It's okay, really.'

'No, let me accompany you.'

'Nice old-fashioned word, it goes with my dress. Anyway; why?'

'To quote you: why not?'

'You'll have to do better than that.'

She walked towards the door giving a casual wave, turned and walked away past the windows.

He was aware that he hadn't really noticed their surroundings, his usually precise visual recall pleasantly impaired by her presence. He sat, looking through the plate glass window at shops and houses that seemed rather ordinary and tired and, realising it was merely a projection of himself at this moment, paid and left.

Walking to the station and hearing rap from a large BMW, thinking again how it ruined rhythm and murdered melody, and knowing the mood he was settling into, tried not to be annoyed on the Tube by phone users who didn't realise that the electronic assistance provided meant there was no need to shout to their relatives in Sophia.

He went into his street, noticing as he turned his key in the lock that some putty was cracking in the curved metal frames of his front window, went in and sat behind it, looking out at an evergreen bush and glancing at Simba, a soft toy lion on his phone table given him by an African student. He turned his head towards the French window at the end of the long, greying white lounge and saw his garden. It was overgrown; tall, yellowing grass, the waterfall obscured by ivy, small trees beginning to grow in the rockery from the damsons dropping from above it, and the cracked fountain which hadn't worked for years. It was dry, lifeless, so were the drooping daisies, fence, the trees in neighbouring gardens, the houses on either side of his in the link terrace; he had been here too long.

What was it his ex had said? 'You'll land up an old man with nothing more than a tidy house.' And the girl who had given him the toy had weighed in with, 'To love someone you have to love yourself.' He guessed that to say that all clichés are born of truth was not only simplistic but itself a cliché. He thought of Gail, he liked her name, liked her. He still had no way of contacting her. She didn't even know his name, hadn't asked.

He turned on the radio; a presenter had died and the BBC was looking for a woman to replace him. He imagined the outcry if they'd wanted a man. Way back he'd canvassed for his local Labour party candidate, trying to persuade him to come to his evening class, convinced that all politicians needed at least a basic grounding in social science before they uttered an assumptive, uninformed public word, and been on occasional left wing demos pushing the socialist message to all and sundry, until he realised that the Left seemed to be spawning a liberalism that was mere self-congratulation disguised as humanitarianism rather than a true ideology for the welfare of others,

He decided that as The Jarrow March had long finished its slow journey and 'The Ragged Trousered Philanthropist' had become a coffee table publication, perhaps he would have to settle for theoretical Marxism. Globalization - a value-neutral euphemism meaning the political, economic and exploitative control of the world by multi-national conglomerates - would eventually bring about its own end anyway, though it seemed to be getting there rather slowly, at about the rate the moon was receding from the earth; the speed of fingernails growing.

Before bed, he went up to his office - feeling 'study' rather pretentious, the same thinking ordering him, when at university, to use a Sainsbury's bag to carry his work in - to see if anyone had bothered to send him an email. There was a YouTube message. He glanced at it and was about to switch off, tired of sneezing Pomeranian puppies, babies doing ever cuter things, up-town funk-you-ups and JFK's assassination yet again, when he saw a still of the back of a woman in a shoulder-padded frock holding a mike. He clicked on. The camera eased round to the front of her; it was the 'Blackbird' song smoothly rendered by Gail.

The video also showed close-ups of a trilby-hatted man with a wide tie grinning up at her with rather hungry eyes. He hadn't noticed him in the hall. As she repeated, 'Sugar's sweet so is he, 'another shot showed him emulating a backing chorus of 'tchoo tchoo tchoo, tchoo tchoo,' moving his upper body as if he was in Mo'town.

It irritated him. Who was he? How come it had been put online so quickly? He knew it shouldn't have mattered, he'd only seen her twice. But it did. He went to bed feeling a little dulled.

As soon as he woke he thought he would look for her, although concomitant with this was the feeling that it was not only infantile but pretty pointless. Yet, perhaps this was the project he needed. It was hardly the beginning of a satisfyingly fulfilling intellectual endeavour or a stimulating trek to see the Buddhist temples of Tibet or, better still; wandering around Cuba's remaining Art Deco. He was also bored. He knew what he would be doing over the next term which was almost exactly what he'd done at the beginning of the last academic year.

He didn't feel like painting or sketching anything or, unusually, continue his sporadic walks around London; wandering through N6 and South Kensington or walking the Thames Path to Henley as he'd done a few years previously. Again, he pictured her in the hat and veil, with that unhurried quality she possessed, her eyes having a certain leisurely movement when they changed direction, away from or to him. And her singing; she could have sung a telephone directory, if they still made them, and he would have listened. No, as futile as it seemed, he would search for her.

CHAPTER 2

Billy Raines was on a bus on his way to his favourite cafe in E 3, 'Compotes,' which, because he thought it funny, he called 'Compost' when talking to its Mauritian owner.

'The old play on words, eh, Rihad? Nuffink personal, as a veggie I like your salad and stuff, know what I mean?'

He went upstairs, camera as ever hanging from his shoulder, dropped his baker's boy cap on a table and looked across the road from the narrow window to see if he could spot some totty he fancied and maybe take a shot of. He'd found some the previous week when strolling through Hyde Park and seeing a group of females on a self-styled pin-up parade and asked if he could take some shots. Without waiting for answers he'd begun.

There were those in floral two pieces, a few with gingham tops, one with a peasant blouse, a girl in a one-piece bathing costume, an auburn-haired woman strolling around in an American sailor's hat saluting people and, at the edge of the assembly of the three dozen or so taking part, a cutie in a striped one-piece bathing costume with hair piled high trying too hard to look like Betty Grable. He enjoyed himself. While looking at his shots on the bus home he wondered if he would get some orders from the email addresses he'd acquired; they might just make up for the current surfeit of non-orders from his usual weddings, christenings and funerals trade.

As it was Rihad's turn to host the area's Arts Trail, there were paintings and lithographs by local artists complete with price tags around the walls and the staircase and in half an hour or so there should be some more punters to click his camera at. He looked at the snaps he'd taken in the park again and checked his phone to see if there were responses from any of the people he'd photographed. He'd had none so far and there were none now. One or two of the artists wandered in then more until the room was virtually full, Rihad coming up to move the tables and chairs against a wall to make space.

He wondered where Susie was, she painted a bit, though he wasn't that fond of her stuff, a bit too abstract for him, though he liked the one of a striped beach deckchair with palm trees and a pier in the background. He didn't understand much about abstract paintings but, as she'd said, 'If you've got to stick a label next to one and call it 'A turbulent arabesque of significant complexity' then it's failed.' He wasn't quite sure about the one she had here, it could have been used as a poster for 'The War of The Worlds' and he'd persuaded Rihad to let her put it up though she certainly wasn't a local.

He had another look out and saw the top of a wide-brimmed hat and a pair of open-toed shoes entering the café and, guessing it was her, went downstairs. She was at the counter.

'I thought it was you. Christ, you've got anuvver forties' frock on; you really are taking it seriously aintcha. 'ere, I'll pay for that.'

'No. Many people upstairs?'

'Quite a few.'

He followed her as she took her tea across to a table.

'How is he?'

She looked at him matter-of-factly.

'The same, I think he still recognizes me, though never asks me as he used to if I've made any new friends.'

'Would I be in that category, Susie?'

'Not that new are you, and I have told you not to call me that, its Gail; remember?'

'Okay, just that you look like a Susie, but I still think you're great the way you go to see him every day.'

'Most days.'

'And you don't have to 'cos it don't seem to make much difference.'

'Maybe, but I do see him, so there it is, you know this anyway. Let's leave it, Billy the Spiv.'

'Not many spivs wore Panama hats.'

'It kind of suits you, I suppose.'

'It'd look better on you, darlin'.'

'Sometimes I don't know whether you actually talk like that or you're just playing a role.'

'Nor do I.'

She bent sideways to look up the stairs. 'I came quite a way to put that up.'

'I know, I helped you do it.'

'As a friend should.'

'Only a friend?'

'You know the answer to that.'

'Wanna laugh? I saw this sort yesterday with long legs, though not so skinny that you had to tie her legs in knots to make knees, and I thought she'd have to attach bottles of water half way up 'em 'cos by the time I got up to 'er knickers I'd be lickin' so 'ard I'd run out of spittle.'

'That's disgusting.'

'But you usually enjoy these bits of hyperbole. I like watching you laugh.'

'Not today.'

'Where d'you disappear to at that club the other evenin', anyway? I thought we could have had a drink or something after.'

'You didn't go there just for me.'

'I know, but I thought we were there ... together, as it were.'

'You thought wrong, Billy, let's talk about something else.'

'Could talk about another tie I bought down Brick Lane.'

'Or not. It seems to be getting desperately trendy there,'

'You're an iconoclast, Gail.'

'Didn't know you knew words like that, Billy.'

'There's a few more where that comes from, know what I mean? And I dunno why you didn't bovver to tell me 'bout that Essex do.'

'I just couldn't imagine you outside the parameters of Aldgate Pump and the River Lea.'

She glanced around again. 'Look, I don't think anyone's going to buy it and Rihad will let you know if it does sell.' She rose.

'Goin' already? You just got here. It's 'im again, ain'it.'

She stood. 'Of course.'

'That bag looks a bit periodish.'

'It is. See you, I suppose.'

He sat there watching her leave and musing on when he would see her next. He went upstairs again to take some more shots of artists and paintings, hoping he'd do better business than he'd done at the Park. He thought about the funeral he was going to the next day to take some photographs. The families didn't always know what they wanted so he would suggest a few things: shots of the house, wreaths, flowers, the wake, the guests and, if they were pleased, take photos of the house and maybe some possessions: the chair their father used to sit in, an antique mirror perhaps, his bookshelves. He knew that after a short while the pictures would be put away and rarely seen again, but better, he thought, to have photos they didn't look at and are put away in drawers than regretting photos that were never taken.

She drove to Walham in less than an hour, but it was long enough. It would be easier if she could have him nearer home Instead of close to Colchester. The few nursing homes she had seen seemed just the same as each other and just as expensive. Her visits were a concretised ritual now; she felt she should have her own parking space.

'Hello Mrs. Leonards,' greeted Anisa the Trinidadian nurse, as she entered. She nodded to her and climbed the stairs to his third floor room. She looked at the Adams ceiling at the top of the stair well, the dark, lozenge-shaped floor tiles on the landings, the heavy horn scrolls on the top corners of the door surrounds and wondered if he was aware of the Gothic oppressiveness of it all.

From habit she tapped on the door of his room knowing there would be no response. She pushed it; it was heavy and moved slowly - she felt, as she had before, that it was like a cell door, an impression only slightly diluted by the black painted picture rails, floral carpet and purple curtains.

He was sitting on the arm of a large armchair, the back of his head still as he looked at the framed photos she'd placed on the mantelshelf in front of him. There was one of his mother and father, a black and white portrait of his grandparents, and one of their own wedding; she in a classic white gown, he in a double-breasted suit which, because of his lanky frame, looked a little as if the material was hanging there waiting to be made into a jacket; they'd joked about it.

She wondered how long he'd been staring at the pictures. What was he seeing in them? Was he seeing them? Would he notice if she left the room? It hadn't always been like this of course, but she seemed to be gradually forgetting that time. She leant her back against the door and glanced around, there was so little of him here; a small wardrobe with some of his clothes, the rest were back at the cottage, some books which she knew he hadn't read and probably would never do, and the photos.

It seemed only slightly ridiculous to her now that it was the lean face, wide, full-lipped mouth and the floppy fair hair that had attracted her; a face that fitted his casual charm perfectly. She was aware when they'd first met, at somebody's wedding, that it was easy to be at ease with the world if your part in it had been made easy for you.

His father had been a hedge fund manager, his only son following and moving into and around the corporate arena, though perhaps somewhat less successfully. She'd never been exactly sure what he'd done, only what he'd done for her: introducing her to a life in London, to people she wouldn't otherwise have met, good restaurants, the theatre, occasionally the opera, though often aware that his friends and colleagues and, at times, himself, saw them as commodities to drop superior asides about, to trade within a quasi-intellectual status market. She realised more fully now that she had been a recipient, a willing one and, ostensibly, had done little, just gone along with it all.

She moved sideways a step so she could see his face in the centre of the baroque mirror above the mantelpiece, seeing her own rather wan, seemingly disinterested one. He seemed to notice something and moved his eyes towards the mirror, gazing at her without expression, frowning then moving his mouth a little, perhaps trying to smile. She stood behind him and put her hands on his shoulders, squeezing gently, then bent and kissed the top of his head.

He continued looking in the mirror at her. She took a packet of liquorice sticks from her bag; he'd liked them since a boy and was one of the few things that put a light in his eyes. 'The older we get the more like we used to be, we become.' her mother used to say to her. Carrying that to a logical conclusion, perhaps he would have enjoyed crawling on the floor eagerly discovering bits of the world around him and having his nappies changed, not that he wore them but, according to Alicia, given his condition it could happen at any time. He placed a stick in the corner of his mouth, sucked it and looked at her, frowning again. He usually recognised her, but when he didn't she wasn't quite as sad as when the non-recognition had first occurred. It had made her feel frightened, reminding her that she had depended on him for so much.

Opening her bag she told him she'd bought him a photograph.

'I found it at the bottom of a drawer; you'd think it would have made itself seen by now wouldn't you.'

The healthy man she'd known would have gently mentioned that she was being anthropomorphic. It showed a stocky man and a tall woman holding a baby and smiling at the camera. She wore a mini-skirt and sandals and he, flared corduroy jeans and a spearpoint collar shirt with prints of small cars on it. She held it in front of his face.

'It's you and your dad and mum in their garden, Charles and Andrea. Yes? Remember those large conifers and the gazebo?'

His non-expression was unchanging.

'Ischemic cerebrovascular insult' was a phrase she had lived with for a long while. It had happened suddenly and quietly after a meal of liver, bacon and mash. He had smiled across the table at her, rubbed his tummy, looked down at his plate and remained steadily looking at it. She thought he'd been joking at first but as the time stretched, changed her mind. She'd spoken his name then said it louder and stood up to go to him. His head had fallen forward, a small piece of bacon rind sticking to his hair.

She had pulled his head up. His eyes were open, but seemed to have faded to a pale blue, as if a gloss door had been painted over in matt. She went around to the front of him, took his face in her hands and attempted to shake it, but couldn't make herself do so. She moved the plate, gently let go of him and rang treble nine from the hall. Back in the dining room she walked around it looking at him, not knowing what to do. She shook herself and opened the front door. She left it open, went back to the room and looked at him again, feeling useless.

They came quickly: two men wearing green shirts, one carrying an oxygen mask and some kind of machine. One of them asked her how long he had been like this. While the mask was put over Stanley's mouth the other man returned to the ambulance and brought out some sort of chair which they'd sat their patient in and carried carefully back to the vehicle. She grabbed a coat and sat opposite him as the doors were closed. She felt she should have been sitting there only as an aftermath of a calamitous, noisy accident: a wall collapsing, his car colliding with another, a fall from a ladder, but this was a silent, noiseless anticlimax. The paramedic, without turning to her, told her that it looked like a stroke.

She was feeling on her own, there were no friends here, she had few and there was no family, her parents having her late and dying within months of each other a few years ago, and no children. She couldn't conceive and Stanley hadn't wanted her to have fertility treatment. She hadn't really objected; he was enough, or so it had seemed until this moment. She looked at him more intensely; he was very pale, his skin appearing to be on the verge of becoming diaphanous.

The vehicle stopped, the driver opening its back doors and helping his colleague carry her husband out. She walked with them into the A & E department where they quickly turned along a corridor towards a room at the end which she wasn't allowed to enter, a nurse pointing her to a nearby bench. She sat, feeling almost disembodied.

Seeing a quadrangle outside with flower beds she walked around it. Oh, Lord, what would happen? She had nothing to fall back on, had never really done anything. She had a minor counselling qualification which she'd never used despite Stanley's encouragement - though, suddenly freeing a notion she hadn't visited for years, admitted to herself that perhaps it was a half-hearted urging, that he was happier with her in quiet domesticity - but that was all. She wanted to be in it now, serving him something, but not liver and bacon.

Returning to the corridor, she stood staring at a blank wall in front of her, images and memories of Stanley pouring over it as if a projector was behind her. One, crystal clear, was of him in a suit and tie from the early days, a shoulder-padded jacket making such a difference to his narrow shoulders, another from when they'd first bought the London flat, his parents generously adding to the deposit, and he with an old bellows camera he'd bought somewhere taking a photo of her sitting on a box grinning up at him after the removal men had gone; and holding her so tightly when her mother had died. But these were pieces of virtual imagery, a cyberspace, the real man; the funny, likeable, quietly content man was behind the nearby doors getting stronger, better. Wasn't he?

It was quiet, no nurses or patients, no people waiting to see any of the latter, except her. She'd noticed the 'Emergency Room' sign above the double doors. The first word could have been replaced by 'blablib' for all the meaning it seemed to have till she thought of the people inside giving injections, hurrying, applying things; bandages, splints, bending over and pushing down hard on a chest, his chest.

She was thirsty, almost about to say 'let's have a cuppa' to him and had a quick picture of them sitting in the hospital cafe talking about how they disliked hospitals; the smells, the enforced stays, the neutrality of them. She walked back to the bench again and as she passed the doors, a nurse came out of them and told her that he seemed to be responding, but that she couldn't see him and suggested she go to the cafeteria and try not to worry.

The sweet tea helped, though she felt herself sinking lower into the nothingness of the franchised coffee bar, bland paintings askew on the wall, people at the tables laughing, the elderly women cackling loudly. She got up and hurried back to the now familiar corridor. As she sat restlessly on her bench a doctor came towards her, beckoned her to follow him and went into a room at the other end of the passage, not looking back at her.

Sitting at a desk he pointed to a chair opposite and, trying not to use his restricted medical code, explained as best he could what had happened to her partner.

'You mean a persistent vegetative state,' she'd said as if she'd been a medical student answering a question. She'd recalled the phrase clearly, a detached visuality that, for a second, had pushed away the impact of his words.

'We call it, it seems more ethical, 'unresponsive wakefulness syndrome' now, but it's a little too early to be sure.'

Through her numbing shock she felt annoyance. Did it matter about name changes?

'He's sick,' she said, hearing her voice rising, 'call it what you like, it's real isn't it? It's happened.' She calmed herself. 'Will he get better?'

He attempted to be comforting. 'I'm sorry Mrs. Leonards, we really are doing all we can, he's being moved to ITU as we speak.'

'What's that?'

'It used to be Intensive Care.'

'Another name for the same thing then?'

'Yes.' He looked at her carefully. 'It's a shock, isn't it, there was no warning I assume.'

'No.'

He rose. 'We'll let you see him in a while, but not for long.'

They walked back alongside each other silently until he told her he had another case and left her to the same nurse who took her though more double doors to the unit. As she looked at Stanley lying in a kind of space-age sarcophagus, the distancing came again, the escaping detachment as she asked the names of cables, tubes and computer-like gadgets.

'That's for nutrients,' the nurse replied, pointing to a bag of clear fluid with a tube leading to her husband's chest. She pointed to monitors, suction equipment, a pulse oximeter, ECG electrodes, her listener nodding as if she were a visitor on a tour.

'What's happening then?'

'We're giving him nourishment as you can see, helping him breathe. He'll be here for a while, quite a while I should think.'

She forced herself to ask whether his brain was damaged, picturing it; its two halves, the cortex, temporal lobe. But it wasn't *his* brain, his brain was alright, he was clever, always had been. He could recall almost a whole scene from a play after seeing it just once, remember who had scored how many tries in his local team's rugby games over the last two seasons, knew mathematical formulae for economic predictions; no, his mind would continue impressing her in that casual, grinning way he had.

'You can sit with him a little while, but only ten minutes I'm afraid.'

A chair was slid across to her and she sat again, the nurse busying herself behind her. She leant over and looked at him, he was breathing evenly, his skin colour dusty and drab, the nostrils more flared than usual. She wanted to touch him, wake him, tell him not to be so lazy, he had things to do; mowing the lawn, sitting next to her in a cinema, ordering a meal in a pub, being home, being with her. Kaleidoscopic pictures rotated in her head and settled strangely into one: a picnic they'd had when he was driving them to Bath.

She didn't really like picnics and wasn't aware he'd made a packed one and put it in the boot. He'd stopped the car at the side of an A road, took the food over to the grass border around the high wall of a manor house and told her to come and sit down as he spread a table cloth and started humming a few lines from 'Blanket On The Ground.' She didn't think he liked country music. It was a trivial moment, unimportant, yet there had been so many like it; ordinary, pleasant insignificant, and they heaped up inside her suddenly into one huge bunch. She bit her lip to stop herself crying.

'You need to go now Mrs. Leonards, I'm sorry.'

'Can I stay in the hospital?'

'It's up to you of course, but it may be better if you were with a friend or someone in the family, he's in good hands.'

At that moment the doctor came into the room, smiling briefly at her and walking towards his patient, casually leaning towards him, not looking at her.

'The clot seems to be reducing, but we're not really sure, we'll have to see what happens when the pressure eases. There's nothing more to do, it's a matter of time and I don't know what amount of that commodity is needed to make any significant change. The best thing is for us to contact you.'

The nurse gestured for her to leave. As she did she watched for a second the man's white-coated back bending over her husband, and closed the door. She went out of the building past the ambulances; the driver of one of them, laughing with a hospital worker, had bought her and Stanley in. He caught her eye but didn't seem to recognise her. It was so everyday, pragmatic; ordinary. She'd got a taxi home.

There, she went into the dining room, kitchen, the living room, upstairs to the bedroom and of course he wasn't there. She turned to go down and out again, to make her way back to him but, forcing herself to realise there was no point, removed her jacket and sat by the phone in the hall.

She thought of the paucity of friends again: there was Becky, Jenny and Jacqui and, she supposed, the 'cheeky chappie' as she sometimes called Billy to herself and who she'd known only a few weeks, with the eternal camera which he'd grab every few moments to take a shot of a shop doorway, perhaps a tree leaning from a pavement, a piece of period crockery in a charity shop, or a picture of her if she wasn't quick enough to stop him.

As she looked, now, at her partner's grey face, the light in his eyes as faint as it was twelve months ago when it had suddenly dulled, she knew there was little point in coming, but the pointless trek had been institutionalised and as she glanced at the unchanging, mute features of the room she felt it was herself that had become so, that she couldn't do without the almost daily experience of Leyland House. But not tomorrow.

Becky had shown her a leaflet urging anyone interested to attend a local demonstration continuing the work of protesting mothers who'd been evicted from a local hostel and told they would be sent away from the capital while there were, apparently, decent but boarded-up houses empty in the next street. It was the downside of gentrification, a word she thought inappropriate, liking Billy's 'snobbing up' better.

Her friend had urged her to come, she could wear her old-fashioned stuff she'd said, it would cheer her up. She needed to do something, something practical, of some use. Stanley would have to do without her the next day but, for him, he had probably done without her for a year. He wouldn't miss her.

CHAPTER 3

He was leaning against the back wall of the classroom, hands in pockets, body arched forward a little, right leg bent, heel resting on top of the skirting and head cocked slightly to one side like his childhood photos. For six months he had been teaching this group the sociology of medicine. Most would go on to a nursing or social work degree. He was doing role-plays with them and had suggested a scenario or two; the Jehovah's Witness parents of a young, injured child who were refusing to allow a life-saving blood transfusion - what would, could, the medical team do? A similar question was posed by a sick menstruating woman being treated by Orthodox Jewish doctors. It was a delight to watch two Igbo Nigerian women and a Kenyan man play the doctors.

With encouragement they'd create their own situations and act out one or two a lesson. They particularly liked making up stories that enabled them to dress up - tongue in cheek he'd suggest nurses' uniforms with fishnet stockings and stiletto heels would be appreciated - and, if they justified it in the context of a genuine ethical dilemma, to use music. The head of department would sometimes look through the door and frown perplexedly at them.

One of them was delivering a baby - a large black doll - from a fair-haired Spanish student, slightly shorter than the doll, lying on a desk surrounded by other 'medical staff' who were laughing and screaming with delight. He liked the innocence, the ingenuous nature of African women, except when it came to religion.

He'd told them, trying to get them to step back from the social world and attempt to look at it detachedly, of European oppression and control through Christianity and that god was either a well-intentioned deity who was obviously not omnipotent, or all-powerful and therefore a bastard or, a third alternative, was both weak and a bastard, and anyway, he didn't create us, we created him. This was predictably met with surprise, anger and, sometimes, pity, though usually after his introductory lecture half the females would, as they passed his desk, squeeze his shoulder and tell him they would pray for him. God was involved in their work, particularly their research projects where, in their acknowledgements, they would thank various organisations and individuals who had helped them, often including the almighty. He'd suggest they put him higher on the list than god. Some took him seriously.

Pulling a chair across he sat down, watching them. Maria was holding her 'new-born' tightly and miming breast-feeding while Charity, the youngest in the class and wearing a stars and stripes headscarf, was jumping up and down with glee. It was she who, after he'd told them that sepia photos of ringed female necks a foot long and 'savages' with bones through their noses had been part of his early upbringing, had insisted to the group that the bones were fashion statements. On her mobile he knew that it permanently said, 'I love Jesus and Jesus loves me.'

It was his last class of the day, though still early, and as a mechanic had taken his car in for an MOT, he'd decided to take a walk before going home. He went along a street he hadn't been down for years that was quintessentially London: Victorian houses, a block of fifties flats, a couple of gabled thirties style houses in place of those destroyed in the Blitz, crudely pollarded pavement plane trees and the ubiquitous wheelie bins with orange tops.

Although he wasn't really enjoying this particular street he idly wondered why he liked looking at houses so much and what they represented; maybe it was the child in him, even the baby. Perhaps bough'd leaves against a window was like a mother's hair touching an infant's face, a cupola could be an offered breast, eaves the brim of a merry widow hat, and the long folds of a full-bosom'd caryatid's skirt was for a child to hide beneath - a strange, exciting protection from the world where a jasmine hedge cushioned his boundaries. But then, the raised eyebrow of a high gable held a kind of intimidation, tall railings were a demand from his father to hold his back up, and a flint chequer patterned wall became the pain of a boy's mishaps.

Pulling himself into the present, he stopped for a coffee in an old workshop that was now a studio-cafe with obligatory eclectic furniture, a metre high plaster tiger atop a corner piano, a bearded man sitting behind a table piled with speakers playing some sixties pop and country, and where folk singers would sometimes entertain by singing through their nose by ear. In the loo a yellowing front page copy of an old newspaper stuck on the wall with a photo of Tate and Lyle's sugar girls made him think of Gail.

Deciding not to go home he went straight to where he'd last seen her, the club, realising as he entered he should have rung first in case it was closed or there was no one there to give him the information he wanted. It was open but, not seeing anyone, he walked into the hall, fancying he could still hear her singing, 'No one here can love or understand me, Oh what ... ' A voice behind him asked if its owner could be of help; it was the manager. He remembered the girl but had no idea who she was, though supplied the name of the band and its phone number and thought it may have a website.

vincent thanked him, left the place and went back on a train watching a man at the end of the carriage shouting into his phone and eating hot food, oblivious to the idea that the fumes could offend anyone's olfactory senses and, if aware, would probably not have cared anyway. He posited the idea to himself of an inverse relationship between increasing technological sophistication and a reversion to the primitive; we were savages with smartphones.

A woman sitting opposite was assiduously applying make-up; a further example of the distinction between the public and private spheres being rapidly annihilated. He watched her eyes in the solipsistic mirror, the widening gaze to brush the lashes, mascara, the underlining, then narrowing for the rouge, the lipstick gloss, a glimpse of bleached teeth, a comb tweaking a fringe then a powder brush revolving around her face.

He thought of the next logical, crassly indulgent step and imagined her unbuttoning her bra and dropping it on the next seat, then a practised pencil dotting underneath a bared breast and maybe a Stanley knife making an arced incision and a jelly-like mould pushed into the cut followed by a threaded needle with sutures and scissors to finish. The other breast would receive the same treatment and, when completed, it would be the gentle fastening, the deftly gathered tools, mirror; a copy of 'Hello!' and walking out of the opening doors. He could almost see on the floor the forgotten knife, the rolling lipstick half-risen from its holder and, perhaps, a splash of blood.

Back in his office, he found the band's website with a contact address but no telephone number and asked if it, or they, knew who the woman who had sung the other evening at the club in Derrel Road was. He received a reply: No. He looked at the video clip again, it had two thousand hits. The man who kept looking at her seemed to have a familiarity with the place, perhaps somebody would know him. He described him, trying not to turn the description of a long, sallow, grooved face into the bias of a somewhat annoying one. The reply was the same. He wasn't sure what to do.

The next day was a Saturday and he went to one of his favourite cafes in E7, liking it partly because they turned the music down as soon as he entered, he pointing out some time before that if he wanted to dance he'd find a night club. He sat with his food and read till two Caribbean girls came in, one loudly talking to her companion and disturbing his, and others, peace.

Again he idly wondered why foreigners generally, though these could have been born here, spoke louder than the indigenous English. Perhaps it was the weakening of Christianity and its 'do unto others' morality or the fact that as the ruling classes once controlled a large empire, the middle classes felt that they didn't have to shout to be heard; the so-called English diffidence.

One of them demanded 'garlic bu'aah,' the Lithuanian girl behind the counter not understanding. The request was repeated, louder, with her friend telling her it 'didn't ma'aah.' He explained to the waitress what she was being asked for and pointed out to the customer that she couldn't be expected to be understood if she spoke that way. Her glare was received by him with equanimity. He felt at times like King Canute trying to hold back a tidal wave of linguistic horrors. His students weren't like this, at least not in class.

He thought of one of his groups on their first day back after the spring break when he'd tried to tell them about Marx and to sum up his thesis in a sentence.

'Our reality, consciousness, identity, our political, cultural and economic systems are determined by the ways in which we technologically transmute the physical world,' he'd said. 'What do you think then? Is it true? You've got ten seconds to answer.'

They'd looked alarmed, so he'd held his hands out, fingers cupping, encouraging.

'Joke,' he'd said, 'joke.' He'd asked them if they would prefer a story.

'Yes,' one of them had shouted, 'like sitting round a fire telling tales.'

He'd almost seen firelight flickering on their faces. Then they were smiling; Caribbeans, smooth-skinned Somalians, full-faced Ghanaians, gold-bangled Nigerians making their Victorian values heard - not for them the two inch band of flesh at their waist, tops of knickers showing - and the two Dagenham lads who'd asked if the geezer he was talking about was a brother of Groucho. He'd smiled back at them and asked how their holiday had been.

There was a leaflet in the café advertising a classic car and boot sale in Kings Cross the following day. He wasn't interested in cars, but thought there may be a few Cadillacs and Mustangs with fins three metres long and perhaps some people wearing clothes that were fashionable sixty or so years ago that would be of some interest and, of course, perhaps just a chance that she might be there. He went.

He was right about both the vehicles and the garments: there were red and pink Cadillacs, a red drape jacket with leopard skin cuffs worn by a man with co-respondent shoes, Oxford bags hanging from a bloke, with a woman who told him that they re-enacted Pathe film newsreels with a digital camera inside a forties movie one, and racks of clothes where he recognised a Tootal tie and a Van Heusen shirt; not realising he knew such things nor that there was something rather pleasant about them. Two men, looking as if they'd come straight from performing in a Victorian musical hall, rode around on a tandem singing 'Leaning On A Lamppost' while Mexican street food was being served from the side windows of an original Routemaster bus. The strains of 'You made me love you' coming from somewhere made him want to hear her singing it.

After wandering a little longer he saw a man wearing a hat that seemed to shout, 'First World War working class northerner,' the man's Novocastrian accent being a confirmation. Vincent attempted his impression of it with a well-tried 'Yer canna be wearkin' cluss and an ahtist, mun, yer canna,' explaining that he'd heard the lines in a play he'd seen at The National a few years earlier.

The man smiled at him and said, 'I know, I were in cust and it were me who spoke that line, mun,' then added a few more which had followed that one. The serendipity was an instant but brief delight to Vincent and seemed to make the trip worthwhile, even though he hadn't seen the woman he was looking for.

He did little the following week, a dubious highlight being attendance at a short academic course in Charing Cross run by an Examination Board, he telling them of an obviously bright student he had taught who had been failed until his own written protest. They'd apologised.

Feeling restless the day after and calling at a local café, he saw a poster on a wall advertising a Jumble Trail in the nearby 'village,' though this did have some claims to be a little more genuine than estate agents applying the word to clusters of high-rise apartments in the middle of a suburban borough. He ambled around it comparing it with places on the outer edges of London where they left books outside their garden gates. Here were the usual food and community stalls, an increasing number of houses with white louver shutters in front windows and matt finished front doors, but it wasn't really bourgeois country.

He thought he'd get a bus, not caring where it was going like he used to as a child, getting a front seat on the upper deck and looking out from a kind of protective cocoon, watching people strolling, hurrying, shouting; being part of it from a distance. He caught one, the top was full but he got a seat by a window downstairs, noting the architectural periods of shop fronts, a neglected church or two, run-down stretches of property and the area's Victorianism proclaimed by the street names of Roseberry, Ruskin and Gladstone.

They were passing a small park in the centre of which was a crowd of people, mostly, it seemed, women. He got off at the next stop more or less on a whim and walked back, looking through the railings at a banner by the side of the gathering proclaiming in large lettering, 'Focus E15, Social Housing! Not Social Cleansing!' His political antennae aroused, he went in at the main entrance, along with a quick thought that as he was beginning sexual divisions at the start of next term he could maybe use this as an example of current feminist attitudes about protest, and why.

As he drew nearer to them, seemingly organising themselves to move somewhere, a little part of him was asking what more they wanted. They carried life inside them, girls from a young age - their anticipatory roles provided by dolls, dresses and Disney - knew they almost certainly would be and would nurture that life; the hand that rocks the cradle rules the world, women therefore being more emotionally secure than men.

It could be argued, he thought, as he stood watching them, that the feminist debate and its increasing media presence was, like the liberal horror of race discrimination, a smokescreen to take attention away from systematic class-based inequalities. Nobody seemed to shout 'Classist!' in a system of profound inequality. If liberalism was being pushed by the Left, it was, partly, working against itself. He felt a grey cynicism deadening him again. Then he saw her.

She was about sixty metres away at the edge of a group that was slightly separate from the main throng, laughing with the woman next to her. Her hair loosely waved, she wore a shoulder-padded jacket and was playfully swinging a bucket-shaped bag against the legs of her companion. She stopped and looked towards an older woman a few yards away who said loudly and matter-of-factly, 'We know what we're doing, let's go then.'

Just before the rest started moving he looked at her; that lipstick again, her stillness as she watched the speaker. He realised that he would have liked the moment of finding her to have come at the end of an existential chase where he had, perhaps, travelled many miles, seen and questioned lots of people in old pubs, record offices, retro gigs, and in strange places to help him find her, but here she was in a park in East London.

They began to move off towards the main entrance, straggling at first then into a more cohesive body. He wasn't sure where they would go, they couldn't march along the main road unless it had been arranged with local authorities; perhaps they'd just march around the edge of the park. She was towards the front and getting a little too far away from him so he began walking behind. He could see her profile as she turned her head to occasionally look at her companions.

The scene was somehow filmic. He wanted to be with her, holding and swinging their hands together, him grinning, easy, confident, and then a slow zoom-in where they'd be centre frame, space on either side in the crowd, an audience picking them out easily Then a side view of him, head back, laughing into the sun, the camera angling lower, showing his firm jaw followed by a close-up of her stunning profile as he pulled her towards him, ad libbed, improvised...

He was further behind them now and on his own, feeling familiarly that he wasn't of these people; didn't belong. There was a cloud again, descending from inside him, a kind of alienation - the social scientist in him aware it was a concept that hadn't been methodologically operationalized, though he began an idle attempt to do so until realising any analysis of anything at the moment was obscuring the notion that perhaps he'd be rejected by her.

In front of him they were walking through the park gates and spreading onto a wide pavement. He couldn't see her; strangely he felt bereft for a second then saw that it was her now holding up one end of the banner he'd seen. She, with another woman, seemed to be in the lead and heading along the pavement with the others walking six abreast behind them. To the rear of the banner a second had appeared reading: 'Repopulate The Plummers Estate.' He thought there may be objections from people confronted by a stream of marchers coming towards them or from behind, but nobody seemed to mind and there were a few affirmative, encouraging nods as people read the banners. They crossed the road at traffic lights, acquiring a few hoots as drivers were held up by the procession, its width now decreasing as it moved towards a narrower pavement.

The marchers turned a corner by the Town Hall, congregating outside while he stood in a gutter, again not seeing her for a few seconds. When he did she was looking away from her banner and talking animatedly with the woman he'd first seen her with in the park.

There were objections from some pedestrians as they had to step off the pavement. A few of the protesters started to chant, 'The Sheriff Robin the poor,' Vincent overhearing someone explaining that it referred to the name of the local Mayor, and as the banners were held high a security guard came out of the building and onto the top of the steps looking confused then annoyed as he shouted rather amateurishly, 'Go away, move on, disperse.'

They didn't. The banners were held higher as their bearers walked towards and up the front steps, turned around in front of the man and held them even higher, obscuring him as the rest of the protesters climbed and spread out across the steps. The man was obviously annoyed now and yelled at them to move off.

As the noise grew he clumsily grabbed the side of the banner Gail was holding, wrenched the pole from her hands and pulled it towards him, stepping back and dragging the other woman nearer him before she let go of it. Gail didn't hesitate and lunged for the pole. She partly succeeded until the man pulled it from her again. It was like a miniature tug-of-war, having an almost childlike quality, until she suddenly pulled her arm back and punched him in the face.

He released the pole, put his hand to his nose and just stared at her. He then grabbed her arm and pulled her towards him, her feet almost leaving the ground. He turned towards the main doors then through them, dragging her with him and slamming them shut. The woman who had been sharing the banner stood there looking at the closed doors, the banner laying half furled on the steps. There was quiet for a while, people not knowing what to do. Vincent did, but unthinkingly. He pushed through the people on the pavement and the protesters on the steps; went towards the doors and yanked them open.

He didn't see her at first. He'd been here before; oil paintings of town hall faces, smug eyes, snug waistcoats and mayoral chains covered in heavy varnish looked down at him. The guard was pushing her back against a wall, shouting at her again. Vincent strode over to him, gripped his shoulders and pulled him away from her.

'She's a woman. Leave her, just leave her.' he shouted.

In a heavy African accent the man told him to get out or he would call the police.

'She should not have struck me.'

He was large, looked Nigerian. Vincent thought it better not to get involved with the police, they were probably aware now of the crowd outside the building and making their presence felt. He asked the guard if there was a side door. The man pointed to one in a corner of the foyer. Vincent looked at her face for the first time.

'You okay?'

She nodded. There was then a loud knocking on the outside of the main doors and a woman's voice saying loudly, 'Hey, let her out, we're entitled to protest, who d'you think you are?'

He cupped her elbow and walked her towards the side door, turning as they reached it to say sarcastically, *'e dupe,'* thanking the guard, guessing he was Yoruba. The response was a non-committal nod, the guard's hand covering his nose again. They went through the door and into a narrow corridor, through another door at its end and down some steps onto a pavement at the side of the building. She turned to him.

'Thanks. It was good of you.'

'You do remember me, don't you?' He'd hesitated slightly before asking in case she didn't. 'We had a meal together.'

'Yes.'

'You hit him.'

'Yes, I've never done that before to anyone.'

'You could have fooled me.'

'You were a little aggressive, too. I'm glad you were.'

'Guess I haven't done anything like that since I was a kid. Are you sure you're alright? You don't know my name do you.'

'You never gave it to me.'

'You never asked.'

Just then he heard, 'There she is,' and a woman came towards them from the huddle of people at the front corner, looking concerned.

'I'm fine,' said Gail.

The woman demanded she go back to the others with her and took hold of her arm. They went quickly away, Gail hastily looking back to him, silently mouthing, 'Thanks again.'

He watched her disappear around the corner. He stood there; it seemed so odd. She'd gone again. He went to the corner; a few policemen had joined the crowd now, he could hear them telling people to get back on the pavement and move on, no more than three abreast, repeatedly using, 'in an orderly fashion.' He couldn't see her. A few yards away two police cars stopped, more constables getting out of them.

Looking around again he saw a cab stop across the road and Gail, along with the woman he'd first seen her with in the park, easing into it. He watched it as it drove off feeling rather ridiculous and that something had been taken away from him.

He walked amongst the still chanting protesters to see if he could spot the woman who had taken Gail away. He did, and asked if she knew her or the woman who had got into the cab with her. She didn't, had never seen them before today.

'They weren't activists,' she said, before moving away with the chanters.

Rather than an existential thriller, his expedition seemed to be turning into a Feydeau farce.

CHAPTER 4

Stepping out of his narrow, three-storey house, Billy pulled the strap of his camera so it sat a little more comfortably on his shoulder, trying unsuccessfully to ignore the weeds growing from his paved front garden and telling himself unconvincingly that he'd pull them up when his back felt better. It wasn't much of a place, he knew that, but valued what was in it, namely his fifties collection: kitchen chairs of various hues, light shades - some of which were in use, others stacked on the floor - two brightly colour-splotched settees, a record cabinet with piles of vinyl and, especially, fifties clothes.

Two full wardrobes took up disproportionate space, jackets and other apparel were draped over chairs and the rest hung in random places in zipped covers: three-button Italian jackets, double-breasted suits, raglan macks, Crombie overcoats and hats on coat hooks and pairs of winkle picker shoes. There were a few Art Deco objects: miniature perfume bottles, posters, crockery, and stepped photo frames. He was familiar with all the piles and puddles and knew exactly what was in them.

He was going to Soho, near to where he'd had his only full-time job, to collect a Zeiss Ikon camera he'd had repaired. He would also go to a tailor he knew to put an extra buttonhole in a shirt so he could wear his Stratton cufflinks. He'd been increasingly dabbling in photography and, having received a reasonable redundancy sum when the company he was working for as an audit clerk had shed half its staff, had paid off his mortgage and decided to take it up full time. It hadn't been easy; a largish deposit for a wedding commission in six months time which had been paid into his account the previous day, constituted a minor triumph.

He liked going to Soho; shots of it during the fifties of ranks of parked Vespas, neon-signed striptease clubs, the 'Heaven and Hell Coffee Lounge,' the '2 I's,' 'Wheelers' and the 'French Pub' represented a lingering wish-fulfilment.

He would have liked Gail to have come with him, not a very exciting trip but he would have amused her; he liked making her laugh though it wasn't always easy, she seemed to look down quite a bit when, rarely, they were walking together; she didn't seem to be with him sometimes. He should, he supposed, keep his language a little cleaner but adrenaline started pumping when she was with him and he couldn't help himself sometimes.

At their second meeting he'd said to her, 'Have you noticed that the parents who complain loudest about paedophiles are those who have kids no one would *want* to shag?' He was about to add, 'I lie. I'd shag anything,' but stopped himself. He wasn't sure why she seemed to take him seriously. He'd tried a different tack.

'What did the inflatable teacher in the inflatable school say to the inflatable schoolboy the day after he'd given him a pin? 'You've let me down, you've let the school down, and above all... ' She'd laughed at that one, well, smiled.

He'd first met her when looking at an exhibition of London street scenes of the fifties at the National Portrait Gallery and she'd been sitting on a bench looking at some of the grainy black-and-white photos of a girl blowing a kiss to a man as he jumped into a train carriage, and a dog and an ice cream van on an empty Battersea Bridge as if taken by a cockney Robert Doisneau.

When he'd asked her - but not before taking a three-quarter shot of her from behind - if she was interested in photography or had just come in out of the rain, she told him it was partly both. He'd asked her if she'd had tea and, if not, if she fancied the café downstairs. She'd hesitated so long he wondered if she was going to answer at all but then said okay, stood up - she was taller than he thought - and went with him.

She let him pay for a scone and tea and sat opposite him. Averse to anyone looking so sad he went into his cheeky chappie routine to try to cheer her up. It seemed to work for a while then when she mentioned the paintings in the gallery he started talking about photography, feeling on surer ground

There'd been something about her, maybe the cheek bones, the mouth, an almost Ava Gardner quality. He used to fantasise when a teenager about meeting the star at Stepney Green station standing bemused and lost in the dark and he not recognising her.

He would go across to her asking if she needed help. 'Oh, thanks,' she'd say with a smile that sent startled neurons crashing around insanely inside him as he realised who it was. He'd look at her eyes and the cynical little man on his shoulder, telling him that she was merely another human amongst the several billion on earth, fell to the ground and died.

She'd tell him she'd intended to go to Pinewood Studios and that she didn't feel well. He would guide her the few yards to the entrance hardly believing he was actually touching her. Telling her she had come the opposite way and was in East London, she'd lean against the entrance doors, a hand on her forehead. A hidden part of childhood had treacled over him: not being well meant mum's healing fussiness. He'd found a phone booth, called a taxi and was soon ushering her quietly into his parents house - they were in bed - telling her that she could have his room for the night, he sleeping in the spare one.

He would sleep little, thinking of coal mines, tractors, washing up, anything but her lying in his bed directly beneath him, perhaps sleeping naked. In the morning he'd knock on her door, which opened immediately as if she'd been standing, waiting.

'Good morning,' she'd say with a bright smile, no make-up, hair pinned back and indigo high-heeled shoes matching her dress. She felt better and asked him his name. He told her, and heard himself saying that hers was Ava Lavina Gardner before the studios shortened it. It impressed her.

He would lead her into the dining room where his mother looked alarmed till he introduced her as a friend and was greeted with, 'Pleased to meet you I'm sure,' and his dad in his best cockney with, ''ello ducks,' halfway to his seat again wanting to get back to his paper. Neither knew who she was. Mum would cook her bacon, eggs and tomatoes, which Ava pronounced 'tamaytas,' and while she ate he would think of her leaving the pool with wet hair clinging to her face in 'Pandora and the Flying Dutchman.' And here she was in Pelly Road, Stepney, with him.

When she had to leave he would walk to the station with her, watching her on the platform looking back up the rails at an incoming train. Before boarding it she would give him a quick kiss on the cheek an inch from his mouth and say, smiling right into him, 'Thanks again, blue eyes.'

He'd walk back home imagining them - a fantasy within a fantasy - walking into the British Legion with all its regulars; Charlie and Tom propping up the bar, Elsie and Doll in their high-heeled shoes, and the ribbons of gold tinsel either end of the stage. He would smooth them along, a slide here, a spin there, and she would throw her head back, laughing, glitter ball glints sparkling in her eyes. He'd punch the air, silently mouthing, 'I met Ava fuckin' Gardner!' He smiled to himself, wondering why he had made his scenario so chaste.

But this wasn't a Hollywood paragon he was sitting opposite, this was an attractive woman enjoying her tea, though rather awkwardly and not talking much. She'd got up suddenly.

'Look, er, thanks for getting this, I'll accept gracefully, but I want to go now and look at the portraits.' She'd turned away. 'All the best.' she'd said, heading for the door.

'I'll come with - '

He stopped himself; he felt she'd see him like a dog begging. He'd finished his coffee and sat for a while then wandered around looking at some portraits of post-war British actresses. He went outside, crossed the road to St. Martin's, took a few shots, had another tea in its crypt, and out past the Gallery where he saw her leaving it.

''ello, I'm not stalking you, honest.'

He'd asked if it was okay to walk with her to a station or bus stop. They'd walked to Leicester Square and travelled to Liverpool Street. Again, she wasn't very talkative, he discovering little more than that she lived in Mersea. She thanked him again at the station, walked off along the platform and waited for her train.

He saw her again a few weeks later upstairs at Rihad's.

'Hey, what you doing here? What a coincidence, eh?' he said, raising his arms in a stereotypical Yiddish manner. Having lived amongst Jewish families for most of his life he sometimes couldn't help himself:

'This bloke goes into a bar and sits next to a woman and orders a glass of champagne, noticing that she's drinking it too. 'This is a special day for me,' he says, 'I'm celebrating. 'Me too,' says the woman. They clink glasses and he asks what she's celebrating.' 'My husband and I have been trying for a child; today my gynaecologist tells me I'm pregnant.' 'What a coincidence, I'm a chicken farmer and for years my hens have been infertile; today, they're finally fertile.' 'Wow, how'd they become fertile?' she asks. 'I switched cocks,' he says. 'What a coincidence,' she says.'

He knew half way through that he should have halted, but couldn't seem to.

'Sorry, but it's just nice to see you. What you doing here?'

She'd frowned and told him she'd been waiting for a friend.

He'd seen her occasionally since, mostly when she was meeting her pal in the café and feeling that she would sooner be with her only than the three of them together. But he'd won her friend over and had sat with them increasingly longer before they would depart and, once, when her mate hadn't turned up, went with Gail to a cinema. The film was a sad one; hence it may have been the trigger for her telling him about her husband. He understood her sadness then.

When Becky told him that her pal painted, he mentioned the coming arts event in the café and that she could, perhaps, show her work there. Getting Rihad to overcome the 'local artists' stipulation, he'd encouraged her and then helped hang the one she'd bought with her. It was the largest painting there. He wasn't interested in art, but if it could get her more interested in him, all the better.

And there was the club he'd told her about. He was glad she'd come, not bothering to chat to people with his usual bonhomie he'd stood and watched her, He was surprised when she'd got up on stage and sung. What she wore wasn't his decade of sartorial interest, but she could have worn a tin hat and a tepee and looked good. He hadn't much liked the bloke she was talking to and who had left the place with her.

After popping into a flower shop in Dean Street, giving out his business card to the owner, he collected the camera, had a quick walk along Wardour Street where he'd started a film studies course some years before until finding it a bit too academic, and returned home. He was going to a bash in the evening, the last club night under its present organisers, and wasn't sure whether to be street-sharp - American-style two button flecked box jacket with patch pockets and loafers or an open-necked gabardine shirt and Hollywood belted jacket - or a tux. He remembered going to clubs and dances in Camden with his old girl friend and walking behind her using her body as a wind break to protect his quiff. He still had one, some grey hairs now but the tonsorial mode hadn't changed.

Having decided on his first choice, and picking up his big Nikon because he intended to take a 'shitload of pics,' he got a bus to Dagenham and a bar room in a run-down hotel-cum-pub behind its Teutonic civic centre, hearing the DJ's 'Gone, Gone Gone' as he entered. Pearl and George were there as were Jilly, Tracy and Lil, all with a bit of rockabilly gear on: a swing and jive dress, a polka-dot skirt, skull and crossbones shirt, and a flying jacket. He felt, as usual, a little bit too smart, but he liked it that way.

After greeting them all; ''ello me old china, 'ow's things?' 'You alright squire?' 'Jilly, nice to see you, you're lookin' well.' ''ere, George, Charlie told his wife he'd come into some money. 'e told her she could buy anything, do anything, the world was hers. She said she wanted to go somewhere she'd never been before. He said, 'Try the kitchen.' Simon played anything good yet?'

The 'Rock and Roll Trio's, 'Train keep a-rollin,'' came on then and, caught up in the sound, he started bopping where he stood. As one of the women joined him, and the band - guitar, bass, drums and a singer trying his best to look and sound like Eddie Cochrane - got onto the tiny stage, he moved to the middle of the floor, dancing faster and getting down low before he thought he'd better start taking pictures. A friend had pointed out that as he often put his name plus 'professional photographer' across the prints in such a large font he should get the people in group photos to stand on tiptoes as if peering over the letters. But you had to let people know who you were and that it was your copyright; it was his job, he had to make a living.

Retrieving his camera from one of the blokes he'd asked to look after it, he went to the edge of the room focusing mostly on the females, especially those with long legs and well-shaped calves and, occasionally, with feet angling out and back again, spinning on the parquet floor. He moved nearer them shouting 'Say 'bollocks.' to those he knew, snapping them as they laughed. He went to the bar for some food then back to take more photos.

After a final round of DJ music, an ever-present held his hands aloft on the stage asking for quiet then gave a speech thanking their departing hosts for the last three years and wishing them luck for their next venue. There was clapping, raised glasses, the obligatory whoops and then Billy called for them to line up across the front of the stage for the group shot. He posed them as best he could and after proclaiming, 'See yer at the next one, 'ere keep yer eye on 'im, I know what he's like;' he told a quick joke to Pete.

'Two blokes in a bar, one says to the other, 'I made a Freudian slip last night, I was having a meal at me mum's and meant to say, 'Would you pass the butter please,' but it came out as 'You fuckin' bitch, you fuckin' ruined my fuckin' life.''

He left and went home. He'd enjoyed the evening, but would have been happier had Gail had been there.

She heard it from Anisa.

'Mrs. Leonards, I'm so sorry, but your husband's - '

'Dead?' she asked, knowing the answer by the expression on the nurse's face.

'It happened a little while ago, one of the carers went up to give him his meal and he was lying on his bed. She called the doctor. I'm so sorry. I never get used to this happening you know, and he's been with me - '

'It's alright.' Gail said, stepping towards her and giving her a brief cuddle. She put herself on automatic mode and asked if she could see him. She could, but he'd been taken to the small room in the basement. The nurse led the way down the flight of stairs.

'I don't know whether the orderly will be with him.'

She knocked on a shabby, panelled door, the sound echoing. Gail moved in front of her and firmly pushed it open, closing it behind her after turning to give her guide a brief smile. She had never seen a dead person before, including her parents, having no wish to see them in death. He looked precisely the same as he had done since he had been there, just a little paler. She felt she should say something to him but didn't know what, she didn't know what to feel either. Maybe she should feel it now, all of it, not let it overtake her later, fill her, bring her to her knees. She couldn't.

She went closer to him, one eye was slightly open. She put a forefinger on its lid and gently closed it. She'd probably never touched that part of his body with her finger before - with her lips, yes; they had explored most of it. He didn't seem much more of a stranger now than he had when she'd watched him ignoring her as she sat with him in his room. The door opened and an orderly asked her if she had permission to be there.

'I'm his wife.'

'I recognise you now, I'll leave you alone.'

A slight, almost hesitant panic visited her before she made herself think of practicalities: a doctor, though of course he'd been seen by one, funeral directors, letting his relations know, she had a few addresses, friends, associates, a church; he rather liked one in London somewhere but she couldn't remember its name. She ought to tell someone immediately, it was the thing to do, they should know right away, but whom? Although most people she knew seemed to like him there was no special friend. She wondered if, since he'd lived in this place, he had still been himself to himself, though unable to convey it to anyone, to anything. He may have known he was going to die, a few minutes, an hour, a day before he had. The thought of him holding this knowledge made her want to cry. She stopped herself.

She'd read somewhere about grief and ways of dealing with it. She tried to remember. There were the nomads who didn't seem to understand the loss that had affected their lives - she understood, didn't she? - the memorialists who were committed to preserving the memory of the one they had lost, it was coming back now. There were the normalizers, people trying to recreate a sense of family and community, activists helping other people dealing with the same thing that caused their own loved one's death, and those that sought some sort of meaning, philosophical, religious... These weren't her. These were labels put on emotions, things that were felt. No, she wasn't any of these.

Stanley wasn't here any more; his shape was, his still fair hair, long hands, his clothes; shirt, trousers, and his shiny shoes that were always thus; somebody must have dressed him. There was a quiet knock behind her, the door opened.

'Mrs. Leonards; so sorry about this.'

He was a short, rather fat man. 'I'm the doctor here. It was rather unexpected, though there was no pain for him.'

She recognised him from when Stanley first came here.

'How do you know?' she asked. 'Anyway, it's happened. Thank you, I'm sure you did your best.'

'I'll leave you.'

She continued looking at the body; that's what it was now, unoccupied, vacant, a thing. And weren't there supposed to be stages of grief? Denial, anger... or were these for the people who were dying? It didn't matter. There was a huge hole now, but she wasn't going to fall into it, she was going to fill it, make her own life. She would do it.

She turned away, a quick look back, he was so still. She closed the door gently behind her and went up the stairs towards the exit. She didn't wait for the receptionist to say anything. With a little smile she said, 'I'll let you know the funeral arrangements as soon as I know them myself. Thank you.'

As she went out of the building a part of her couldn't quite believe the words she had just spoken, it was an ending; a nothingness. She looked up. For a few seconds the trees seemed to spin around her like a hackneyed camera sequence in a movie. She straightened her back and continued walking.

CHAPTER 5

Vincent was a little annoyed. He'd been on his way to a book launch - his working class roots writhing at that last word, filling him with images of Home Counties public school complacency, pseudo-intellectualism and the taken-for-granted expectational norms of childhoods so different from his own - and, trying to convince himself that the mundane had a significance, had broken his journey at a local high street and bought a pair of insoles. On his way back to the station he'd picked up a free newspaper on top of a pile outside and inadvertently dropped his purchase, not realising until on a platform that he'd had done so. Returning to retrieve it, a headscarved Romanian woman distributing free newspapers to passers-by, and pointing to him, began wailing to anyone who would listen, especially the young copper leaning against a pavement rail, *'E este de etansare cadoul meu!'* then, her wailing continuing, 'He is stealing present from my friend.'

As the concerned constable looked at her, she repeated her accusation. Thinking that she wouldn't understand, Vincent briefly explained to the officer that he had bought them, and was turning to go when the latter asked him if he had proof of purchase. Vincent invited him to return to the nearby shoe shop with him, on the way chatting amicably but not mentioning the purpose of their walk. Obtaining a written statement from the assistant they went back to the station where the officer tried to explain to the complainant who, while still loudly lamenting, continued distributing her papers. He couldn't be bothered to wait around and caught his train.

It was on the second floor of a pub in the West End. He was late. In a long, narrow room with coloured, leaded-glass windows and a bar were fifty people: a malice of poets, a swirl of grey-haired men, asexual Germaine Greer and Judie Dench look-alikes, Oxbridge and casually slumming, and all rather expensively dressed. He'd come to see an old friend who he hadn't seen since they'd both read their poetry at an extramural event at the L.S.E. two years previously. With her bulging bob of black hair and neatly cut fringe she reminded him of a page boy at the court of one of the Henrys. She had wide hips and was standing, jeaned legs apart, at right angles to the bar with an almost beatific smile from her large teeth. She was a lawyer and as she saw him they both said, as if orchestrated, 'Scientists use lawyers instead of rats now; 'cos you can get too close to rats and there's some things even rats won't do.'

She laughed, kissed his cheek then turned to someone who shouted 'Jilly!' and who gave her a crushing hug. The recipient raised an eyebrow at Vincent, signalling, he assumed, that she wouldn't be spending much time with him this evening, further confirmed when a long-haired man with a Welsh lilt said hello to her and to whom she turned with outstretched arms. One of the support poets started reading. He heard 'fecund land,' a line later 'soul,' then an adjectival glut and some neo-surrealist poetry dwelling in its own arse. Jilly had disappeared inside a huddle of pearls and Chanel, but he could email her tomorrow.

The more he saw and heard poets read their work the more convinced he was that their presence in the enjoyment and appreciation of poetry was unnecessary; the reading of a poem was merely an audio version of the real thing: the elemental relationship between writer, reader and the written word.

Half way down the stairs was a toilet; a mixture of urine stench, the sound of a turbo jet drier and, from a speaker embedded in the ceiling over a cubicle, the quiet, slow, insistent: 'Say, English, *Ingles,* Say, do you understand? *Entiendes?* Say, you do not understand. *No intiendo.* Say, do you speak Spanish? *Hable Espaniol?*'

It was mesmeric, its seeming randomness fascinating him, soothing the bludgeoning, self conscious erudition of the poetry a few moments before. He read little himself now, not even when he'd run his own poetry venues.

The first had been in Borough Market, a second floor room in a Georgian house above a shop, the building vibrating as trains crossed a railway bridge less than six metres away, with the smell of sausages being grilled filling the room from 'Posh Bangers' below. Although the room had, as an American visitor put it, 'the classiest lectern in town,' the fumes had got thicker than the camaraderie and the congregation sparser.

The second had been a pub under London Bridge where he'd got tired of saying to drinkers, 'You can tell me to fuck off if you like, but our guest poet's from Northumberland and it's a long way to come to read in this noise. I've no right to ask you to move, you've come for a drink and you want to enjoy it, but could you move a little further down?'

The last place, an Italian-run coffee shop, he had, upon realising he was tired of watching people read poems especially rhyming ones by those still clinging to their nursery experience, only just given up on. He'd found it while walking around the city: mostly the Dickensian alleyways, Georgian terraces in Spitalfields, the churches, guilds, markets, and half-heartedly looking for the buildings he'd worked in as a young tradesman years before - still hearing Jock the foreman telling him that if the plaster was too wet to prime then, 'blow on it till it's fockin' dry'.

On a crowded train again next day he listened to the English language being splintered into tribal dialects with hoodies grunting sentences made up exclusively of consonants and teenagers gabbling in a quizzical transatlantic 'up-speak' as if, with its crackling vibrato, every sentence, was a question. He suggested to himself that language shouldn't drool like water dribbling from our mouths; our ability to speak remaining our best way of communicating with one another and holding together a frayed society.

Afterwards, on a bus heading westward, he felt the annoyance gradually leave him as he looked out at cream-painted stucco houses, bay windows and established trees in bushy front gardens. He began thinking of what made, controlled, a lessening of an emotion, a diluting of it, what actions of neurons, molecules or whatever they were determined it and, more importantly, what it actually was that felt it, what it was that felt anything; a consciousness. Was it somehow separate, a mind-body dualism or explicable by positing materialism, that it existed in the physical brain, or could we ever know? And what did it mean to 'know'? He realised his anti-science stance was present, preferring the non-material, spiritual even. But could spirituality somehow be also of matter, of the physical... He forced himself to stop the never-ending regress and thought about Gail.

He wasn't sure how to find her now. He'd done research before, mostly of course, academic, though tending to rely on intuitive answers unless they obviously wouldn't do, but he was on unknown ground here. At the moment he felt that he'd have more chance of finding her on Google's instant street views looking out of a pulled-back curtained window or walking around a corner than by anything he could do himself.

Fancying a bit of urban bustle he decided on EC1 again; maybe he'd drop in and see Antonio who'd run the coffee shop and who had walked around Detroit for a week on his own to see if he could create some urban poems from the experience. He wandered around a little then spotted a church which he'd seen before but not been in. Before doing so he ambled around the small cemetery at its rear.

He looked at the winged angel monuments, a testimony to Victorian piousness and order, at the inscriptions - for his own he'd probably settle for, 'Here lies an atheist, all dressed up with nowhere to go' - the names on the mossy headstones, Braithwaite, Dobson, Samuels, the long grass, the wilting flowers, some still in their cellophane wrappings like a strange new Victorianism protecting naked plants from the lascivious eyes of men, and wondered again why he liked graveyards.

It wasn't just the quiet and feeling of peace, underlying these were their social purpose; funerals, ceremonies were rituals and, like many rituals, were comforting, part of order, and order is reassuring; they were a reminder that we continue; a confirmation of our own existence.

Walking around to the front of the building, he saw a horse-drawn hearse stopping outside followed by cars. Some of the people that got out of them wore traditional black, most wearing hats or carrying them as they walked up the wide steps towards the entrance. He didn't really want to see or hear a funeral service, but did want to go inside and, because others were, his curiosity was strengthened.

He sat on the back pews and saw an oak table supporting a flower-strewn coffin with the mourners settling nearby. The last time he'd been near a cremation was when he had done some sub-contract work which involved lying on top of the furnace in a North London crematorium painting the ceiling while one of the men that had done the burning had sifted through hot ashes, found a melted gold tooth and ring and casually pocketed them.

He looked around him. It wasn't precious, no Catholic gold and glitz, just white columns, acanthus leaf, rams horns, dulled oak. He imagined a sparrow looking down on the grey heads, black coats, wheelchairs, a corner painting and tomb, hearing a violin dirge in a square nave that had housed hatreds, saccharin cant, that had never seen a flowered 'Grandpa' nor crossed hammers in claret and blue roses; and this before the spirit's weakening to the body, the fidgets, coughs, desire for the wine and smoked eels, and the toilets. The service began. He listened to the growling organ music for a while then, feeling its oppressiveness and separation from him, quietly left, the heavy doors clanging behind him.

He crossed to a café opposite which he'd been to before and liked, partly because of its variety of baguettes but mostly for its Art Deco feel. The period represented to him the first glimpse of a world outside of the huddled Victorian terraces of his childhood. He'd read detective picture books showing cocktail cabinets and Lalique glass while their real life counterparts lived in his aunt's suntrap window house in Hornchurch. He could see her sunray gate, rockery, the front door's leaded- glass yacht and, inside, the zigzag wallpaper and feeling a, 'don't ask, don't get,' nudge from his mother as he'd swallowed dry cake from a Clarice Cliff plate.

Looking through the window he saw people leaving the church and getting into cars. One was a woman standing a little apart from the others, her hair and top part of her face almost hidden under a veil. He hadn't noticed her in the church. There was something familiar about her. She looked up as an older woman moved towards her and squeezed her arm, a younger one doing the same.

He then realised who the comforted was, though this time she wasn't playing an innocent period role but an obviously real one. She spoke to her companions; they appeared to be surprised at what was said to them. After little hesitations they both embraced her and got into a car, turning their heads towards her as they were driven off.

She turned away and walked westwards. Once more, while she was in his sight, he didn't know what to do. He wanted to follow her, but it seemed so adolescent, a sort of cheating. She was quite a way from him when he started to do so. She went a hundred yards then turned suddenly right as she saw a taxi disgorging a passenger at a corner and hurried towards it. Another car escape, it felt rather ridiculous now.

As it pulled away he saw an empty taxi on the same rank and went quickly towards it, tensely telling its driver to 'Follow that cab.' Hardly believing he'd actually said it, he added a 'Please.' They went towards Farringdon where her cab stopped, he asking his driver, who so far hadn't said a word, to do the same. He watched her go into a café, order at the counter and, as he entered, sit by a window.

Removing her hat and putting it and her bag on the seat beside her, she looked pensive. He seated himself two stools away, waiting for her to look up at him, thinking it less scary for her to see him than for him to suddenly speak to her. She looked out of the window.

'Er, remember me?' He said it quietly, too quietly, she didn't hear him. He spoke a little louder. Her expression was almost one of shock; he'd taken her away from wherever she'd been in her head.

'Sorry, I didn't want to startle you. I was in the church.' She was looking at him now with a slight frown.

'You're probably here because you want to be left alone.'

Perhaps it wasn't wise to tell her that he'd followed her, though perhaps obvious he had. The frown deepened.

'You followed me?'

'Yes, from the church, it was an accident, I mean, seeing you, I was just looking around, at the architecture; I certainly didn't expect to see you of course. Can I do anything? Get you something?'

She shook her head, partly saying no, partly conveying a mild incomprehension.

'I'm sorry for your loss, whoever it was.'

A waitress bought her order. She looked down at her food silently, then, 'My husband, he'd been ill for some time.'

His reaction, though not recognising it immediately, was a feeling of infantile jealousy that she'd been married. He let her be while she continued gazing out the window.

'I wanted to get away from that church, anywhere really, that's why I'm here. It's better here, away from those oleaginous, artificial buggers, relatives, some I'd never seen before. We used to have friends around here, came to this café sometimes.' She fell silent again, picking at her food.

'The last time I watched you eat we were... Look, my name's Vincent. At least you know that now.'

She smiled. 'Yes.' She looked up at him. 'My husband had been ill for so long and I think that's probably why I hit that guard man'

'It doesn't matter now, it's nothing.'

'Perhaps all the frustration of the last year, not being able to do anything, just watching him doing nothing every day, nothing, and stopping me doing anything. Does that sound selfish?'

'No.'

'I did some painting, but not much; I felt, somehow, I didn't have the right to escape even into that. I guess that guard man represented some of that. He had a job to do, it wasn't his fault, but surely we had every right to do what we did. He shouldn't have tried to take the banner away.'

He noticed tears in her eyes then, she was as still as if she'd stopped breathing. He was unsure about comforting her, or how to. He looked around him. Past the counter was a French window then a garden with an old granite wall. At least he could take her there. He touched her arm.

'Come into the garden, it's empty.'

'I thought you were going to say, 'Come into the garden, Maud.'

'That's an old one.'

'My father used to sing it.'

She got up and they went through to the garden. He guided her to some chairs in a corner. She sat turned away from him. Her shoulders began shaking. He put an arm tentatively around them as she bowed her head into her hands and sobbed. He continued holding her, saying and doing nothing until her crying slowly ceased.

'You wanted to be on your own really, didn't you.'

'No, it's okay, I'll be alright.' She reached into her bag.

Without taking his arm away he offered her a tissue, thinking how ridiculous and somehow second-rate it was that 'Pret a Manger' was printed across it. She breathed deeply, held herself upright and wiped her eyes again.

'Well, at least you didn't say that I needed some space.'

'There are worse clichés.'

'You know, I think I should go, I'm tired now.'

He went back inside, got a cab number from someone behind the counter, used it then returned to her, easing her through to the front again.

'I'm glad you were here,' she said to him.

'So am I.'

The car came promptly. After a silent journey to Liverpool Street they walked towards the head of a platform.

'Thanks again,' she said.

He quickly wrote his phone number and email address on a scrap of paper.

'When you're feeling okay again, contact me. If I don't hear from you I'd like to ring you.'

She nodded.

'Want to give me your number then?'

'It's in the directory, under Leonards. I'll be alright; I've only a few minutes to wait. I'll walk up the platform, no need to come with me. Cheerio.'

She held her hand out. He squeezed it.

'Goodbye,' she said, already turning away.

He briefly watched her walk from him.

For him, 'female' meant tall and slim - he was vaguely aware that it was, maybe, because he was frightened of 'buxom,' a woman that was... real. It hadn't occurred to him before. He thought of what his psychoanalyst friend might say to a client who felt similarly; it was a frail ego's fear of giving itself, of trusting it to someone who was tangible, solid - he had a quick image of his ex whose bosom, it seemed, had turned into a galleon in full sail - but then that could be translated into 'mother,' what the baby in every man wanted. The contradictions, he knew would mount, he was also aware that he was dissecting himself again because he didn't want her to get on a train and lose her once more.

The first thing he noticed as he got the Tube home was the smell of fried chicken, and a greasy food wrapper being thrown on the floor of the carriage. He picked it up and dropped it gently into an open bag on the diner's lap.

'I believe this is yours.'

The woman looked confused. He walked through to the next carriage and thought about graveyards and the spectrum of emotions mourners felt at the moment the coffin moved from a decorated facade to the inner workings of heat or earth. He didn't want his own last words to be something like, 'Funny, I keep thinking it's Tuesday.'

At home, trying to relax in his office, he read a little poetry. After reading with, and as host, listening to poets of all shapes, sizes and ideological persuasions, he'd noticed the tendency for female poets to write of the body and the flesh far more than their male counterparts. He knew it could be quantified, though neither exhaustively nor comprehensively, and any conclusions based on the few books he'd recently chosen at random from the collections he'd reviewed for his own publisher, could be seen as vulgarised inductive thinking.

He'd found the ratio of body references - hand/s, belly, eyes, skin, breast/s head/s, neck to be roughly ten to one. Why? It was obviously simplistic to use the 'woman equals nature, man equals culture' view - though whoever thought of this had never worked on building sites or lived on a New Cross council estate - but for men it's 'mother' nature; women as 'other,' the body. Women feed life with it and thus there is the basis for women being more 'bound up' with the body, emotionally, psychologically and physically than men. He recognised that there were also the vested interests of globalised capitalism in the body aesthetic.

Maybe he could turn it into a paper for the London Literary Gazette or something, but knew he wouldn't, he couldn't be bothered. He'd seen her again now; the trip was over. Perhaps another was about to begin.

CHAPTER 6

'I'll make the tea, ain't got no sugar again, but have a bicky. I'll wet yer 'air, ooh, it has got long, I know you like it full at the back but I like it short. If anyone sees you with yer shirt off they'll think I've got a man in 'ere. See in the mirror? Perfick. Ooh, look at all that 'air on the floor.'

Perhaps, he thought, she expected it to be on the ceiling.

'Yeh, we 'ad a nice cuppa tea in Marks, you know, it was lovely, then Sainsbury's, you know, lovely shop, packed with people.'

As if it was a welcome change from its usual lions and wildebeests.

Doris had been cutting Vincent's hair in the kitchen of her home at two monthly intervals for twelve years and was the most vacuous person he'd ever known. Every time he went he'd politely ask her to turn down the sound of her daytime TV soap and if he happened to use a word containing more than three syllables she would ask a deflective, 'What d'you think of the weather, then?' Her son regularly took her on Italian holidays where she hadn't learnt a word of the language. Her *raison d'etre* was shopping.

Vincent wondered why, other than gossip, the working class - that annoying nano-second flick of awareness reminding him that it was a social background he also shared - had so little curiosity. At a house agent's recently he'd asked a girl at the desk why the estate in which they were in the centre of was so popular. Not a word of the Edwardian villas, late Victorian houses or the school, only 'Well… it's nice,' dividing the last word into the estuary 'nie-wess.' He gave Doris a good tip, he always did, perhaps making up for feeling that his irritation with her showed despite efforts to hide it. But there were other reasons for his mood.

The day before, he'd gone to Brick Lane via the main station for some bagels and, walking through the crowded concourse, had suddenly found himself sprawled on the ground. Covering his outstretched arm was a grey jacket, next to it a small pink and black travel bag with wheels and a five foot long extended handle at the end of which a short, podgy woman was frowning down at him.

He'd picked up his sunglasses, placed the jacket on top of the bag and stood. The woman mumbled a reluctant 'Sorry,' and continued walking. A few seconds later at the top of an escalator he politely told her that she could have carried her bag.

'Why should I?'

'Because people can fall over it.'

'It was your fault.'

'Then why apologise?'

She'd lifted her head in the air and strode away off the bottom step on her pneumatic legs. A short time later, visiting Borough Market and walking along Union Street, a motor bike had swung off the car-jammed road and come slowly along the pavement towards him. Vincent had stopped, stood legs apart and spread his arms. The rider had come close up to him and then swerved away with a vehement, 'Fuck off.'

A more specific reason for his disgruntlement was that he hadn't heard from Gail. He was increasingly thinking of her, but there was a guarded element underlying it; he didn't want this to be like the relationship he had had with Nyla.

It had begun in the college refectory. Walking into it, he'd seen at the counter a tall, pale, dark-haired woman with large black eyes, full lips and, though only afterwards did he articulate it, a vulnerable exoticism.

'You look like somebody,' she'd grinned, dropping potatoes onto her plate.

'Actually, I'm Mister Right,' he'd said casually, with what he hoped was a trifling amusement playing around his mouth. As ever, the internal split between the 'I' and the 'me' was active; knowing instantly the impression he was, or thought he was, creating. He'd asked her what she was doing here. She told him she'd just begun a history course. She then guessed his age, less than it was.

'And you are thirty one.' he'd said.

'How d'you know that?' she'd asked with a delight that was almost childlike; an expression, an attitude he came to know well and was constantly affected by and nearly always with an undertow of sadness.

She asked him where he was sitting and he nodded towards the table just inside the door where a student was waiting for him. She sat down with her meal and occasionally glanced across to him. His companion hadn't seemed to notice. He'd taken her that morning to a local social care office where she was prescribed methadone to help her come off heroin. She lived on her own in a banjo-shaped cul-de-sac in the mean maze of an East London council estate and was getting through his course with more help from him than he should have given. He talked to her half-heartedly. Usually, in spite of ten years of teaching, he tended to proselytize as much outside of timetabled hours as within them, but he was distracted by looking at Nyla's table.

It had been a few years since he'd had a relationship, though there always seemed to be some kind of offers from female students to lecturers. He'd been a virgin till he was twenty six and when young he'd wondered what on earth, or in bed, it was really like and had sated himself on mind flicks of skinny Iris at number twelve or the silken, misty space inside the thighs of principal boys his dad had taken him to see at Lyceum pantos.

Next day in the canteen he'd seen her again, asked her out and they were both caught up in a muddled kind of journey. She'd told him she had a sickly ten-year-old daughter who she lived for, and didn't want to worry about or hurt someone else.

'I think we should start off as friends,' she'd said in a rather prim, sensible way. Born and raised in Barbados she'd come to this country at twelve and married at nineteen to a Barbadian whom she'd met in England and who had returned to the Caribbean shortly after their daughter had been born. Asked why she hadn't returned home with her husband she told him she would have been treated as a Caribbean wife.

'I used to lie next to him for months knowing he was seeing other women, but couldn't break free. It was like a chick wanting to get out of an egg and then when it has can only lay beside the broken shell, for comfort, reassurance.'

She would tell him that though she didn't feel she was attractive, people saw her as 'a prize vase that was unobtainable.'

Again, the vulnerability, and the arrogance. She would tell him she'd been thinking of him most of the night but that there was a caveat.

'I'm warning you, you'll fall in love with me. I don't want you to for your sake.'

He believed her, didn't recognise it as projection, a defence. She would announce firmly that she was 'self sufficient' then repeatedly ask on the phone if he'd been thinking of her. 'I just know you have,' she'd preen. Picturing her with chin raised and lashes lowered, he could feel the fragile narcissism.

It was the contradictions: 'I don't want to see you for a while.' she would tell him then say that she'd started waiting by the phone, missing his voice. She went on a work placement for a week and rang constantly. 'It would be fantastic to make love,' she'd say, 'but you'd want more, want commitment, and I couldn't give it.' And, without it feeling at all hackneyed, 'You are my soul.' Next time it was, 'I don't want to share you with anyone, wherever I am I want you to be there,' and 'This is too intense, I'm so scared, I keep wanting to tell you I won't see you again,' and 'I'm unhappy when I'm not with you, I can't breathe.'

Calling him in the early hours, she would say, 'I don't want to put you on the list of people I've hurt.' It's too much, it's all too soon. I haven't been with anyone for seven years. I have to protect myself, wrap my child around me.'

She'd also stated, 'If you don't break your brick walls I'll run away and hide behind mine.' And, towards the end, when she'd said, 'I've been looking for someone to understand me since a child and now I've found you, you live in a cocoon,' he hadn't the will to answer. A few days later she'd rung to say that she would always be grateful to him for helping her.

'Forget you ever met me,' she'd said. 'Don't tell anyone that I'm the bitch that broke your heart.'

A few months afterwards he went into the college as she was leaving it, she seemed taller than ever. She told him she'd come to collect her qualification certificate. She seemed restless; said she had to go. For the briefest moment as she turned to leave he thought he glimpsed a resigned sadness in her eyes. It bought back the whole litany of contradictions: the need, the almost fierce independence, arrogance, possessiveness, wanting to give herself then vanishing into her keep, peering at him through its tiny window. And telling him that when they first met she saw so much sadness behind his eyes she had to turn away, and saying almost disinterestedly as she'd passed him in a corridor outside the college art room, 'Pull me back if I walk away.' He never had.

In the shower he thought of why he hadn't rung Gail. Perhaps he was playing a sort of game, pretending he wasn't really interested or that what interest he had, had gone. 'If you're not going to ring me then I'm not going to ring you, nah nah nanah nah.' This was silly. He wasn't sixteen. He'd ring her.

She had put his stuff away; clothes, ipad, mobile, laptop, but not his books because she'd read most of them with him. Pushing the steps of the loft back up, she went downstairs into the kitchen and looked out of its window at the sloping garden and the tiny piece of sea she could see glinting through the twisted vines above the bench, which looked so empty as if they had never sat on it, read on it, she sketching or casually water-colouring and, sometimes, just listening to the seagulls and gazing across to the distant ramshackle boats stuck on the mud flats.

She could see the flat miles of the Island and the top of the church, also some of the houses on the Coast Road, the old packing shed near the beach and a couple of fishing smacks; and of course the pylons and their gaunt ribs - if she listened she could hear the wires sing. But not the endless poppy fields, bluebell woods, the primrose banks of the streams, nor the golden beaches, they didn't seem that colour anymore. Though to step back in time she could walk down the lane; there was still the salty breeze from the marshes, and the bird calls.

She thought about the will, he'd had a little less money than she'd assumed, though the flat they'd lived at in London was hers now. She hadn't been back there since he became ill. They had tenants who she had, following advice, reluctantly arranged the renting terms for; wistfully thinking that when he was well again they could return to it. She looked at the kitchen, the hall, there was a fair bit of Stanley here, though it was the flat that was more his, she hadn't felt she could assert her own taste and intentions there. But this place was hers and she would now make it more so. The phone rang. It was Billy.

'ello, I wondered how you were, I haven't heard from you since the funeral. How'd it go, okay?'

She asked him what he'd been doing.

'Nothing much, know what I mean. Though I took some shots the other day when a woman invited a few of us from the club for a meal and she said, 'You must have a great camera.' I thanked her for the meal and told her she must have some great pots and pans. Cheek. I'll leave you alone shall I? 'ope to see you in the café then when you can get there. You don't have to stay at Becky's; you can stay with me, I suppose. Sorry. I'll see you. Bye'

As likeable as he was, she sometimes thought he was like a big ball rolling around knocking into things, not knowing or really caring what he was bumping into. She thought of Vincent, somehow his name didn't quite suit him. She supposed she should ring him, but was the impetus to do so because he'd been kind? Was she supposed to respond to him because of that? She didn't know what he did; He'd only given her his name. The phone rang again. It was him.

It was pleasant listening and talking to him though she wasn't really sure why she invited him to her home. It wasn't as if she knew him well, that there was 'anything in it' as her mother would have said, but he had been generous to her, on two occasions, and she didn't feel like travelling, didn't want to see Billy and she could see Becky another time. She wanted a little more time to herself, a continuing recuperation; it was a few days away anyway, and she would take her time getting her own stuff from the loft and make the place hers again.

It wasn't that far from Colchester, he'd left early so that, disliking motorways, he could take minor roads. He had an urge to dramatise the journey, thinking of it as a quest, a goal, even seeing her in terms of pursuit, of quarry - which, in essence, it was - but the landscape was too flat and featureless to satisfy it.

He'd broken his journey to buy some flowers and seen a road sweeper holding his phone and taking a picture of a sofa on a pavement with clothes dumped on it. Was he going to enter it for the Turner Prize?

'I'm reportin' it, it's European stuff or sumfink, mate, I'm always findin' it. You can't say nuffin' though, can yer. The van'll pick it up.' And he trundled his bin away.

Noting this as another example of the suffocating effect of the liberal *weltanschauung,* he asked himself why fly tipping and the casual throwing down of KFC cartons, drink cans and the like, this breaking of public rules, bothered him so much. Perhaps, as a child, he'd seen someone, a friend, an enemy 'get away' with something while he couldn't, wasn't allowed to. Maybe he'd think about it later. He crossed to the Island by the causeway, he knew roughly where he was going, holding an image in his eyes of the map he'd studied beforehand; he had no sat nav.

It was an old cottage, almost a grand one, the front of it clad in white weather boarding with small, gabled attic windows, slightly bowed red-tiled roof, black-painted sashes and a sloping garden. He knocked on the glossy black door, she opened it quite quickly; she looked lovelier than he remembered.

'Hello,' she smiled, 'Come in.'

She beckoned to a room off the hall. He stepped in. It had a picture rail from which hung paintings of deer and hills, sunsets and dawns, and one, full of sensual, sentimentalised Victorian sexuality, of a young girl laying in a bed of white roses, another lying by her side about to kiss her watched by a curly-haired boy peeking from a bush. There were framed pieces of fabric, one with 'Looking Unto Jesus' stitched on, reminding him of a childhood tabernacle with a painting of a tall, blonde, haloed Christ resting his hand on the head of a black boy holding hands with a Chinese girl, the stiff formality of it oozing a contrived, spiritual caring. There was a linen tablecloth with delicately sewn patterns, and a chest of drawers with stencilled trees on the drawers. She asked him if he wanted tea. He nodded almost absently as he looked around him.

'Come to the kitchen with me. How are you?'

The passage had bird-strewn French wallpaper, the large kitchen, painted chairs, a butler's sink, copper taps, a stack of flowered, crinkly-edged plates and two baskets of pot-pouri.

'You like?'

'Very much.'

Realising he still held the flowers he gave them to her. She thanked him.

'What do we do now?'

'Drink your tea. Sit.' He gave a fake bark.

'I'm not ordering you.'

He asked her how long she'd lived here.

'For ever really. 'It was my mother's.'

He gestured to the room. 'This is all you?' She nodded and grinned.

'What do you - '

'Do? Housewifery. Well, I did, but I was thinking of counselling, I'm qualified but never practised. Maybe social work; I don't know.'

'I've just started a course.'

She looked surprised. 'You too?'

'No, I've created it; I know little about the hands-on stuff, the college hasn't done it before.'

'You teach?'

'It's called lecturing, sociology, it's pretty local, mostly mature students. I've never been to this place before. The most easterly inhabited British island.'

She was smiling at him, attracting him even more. He then wondered what the connection was between character and face shape; a receding chin suggesting 'weakness,' a jutting one, 'strength.' How could there possibly be a connection between the shapes of bone growth and... He was aware that this anaemic splodge of irrelevance was a way of blanketing what he was feeling.

'Apparently it is. Taught anything else?'

'I've taught teachers to teach, observed them; assessed them. I've had some amusement too. I've watched pedagogic plumbers, beauticians - 'I teach nails.' I imagined rows of tacks sitting

upright on their chairs - optometrists prattling on about pupils'
pupils and a Sidcup scientist foretelling a microbial apocalypse.'
'What's the most bizarre thing you've observed?'
'A life-sized Barbie with a worn breast getting a kiss-of-life
from trainee paramedics in a flat-tyred ambulance behind a
swimming baths.'
'Want a walk?'
They went outside and opposite to a narrow lane. Usually when
walking he was seeing the sun on London brick or rendered walls,
flashing from a chimney cowl, a window, it was a form of
spirituality; Hampstead, Brakenbury village, Edwardes Square, a
buttress on a Highbury church, a shop awning in Ealing, the Arts
and Crafts of Noel Park, Putney streets, a soft-focused, gentle,
vivid montage of small excitements and peace along canal
towpaths, roads... a trunk load of observations and feelings.

But this was with her, and the country lane, the tops of trees
touching across it making it into a curving tunnel, a slight, salty
taste to the air, thin altocumulus clouds, glimpses of the distant
channel and a certain exciting tenseness was making this, also,
more than an aesthetic experience.

And there was something about the fine scarf she'd thrown
around her throat and the way she walked, her head upright; that
was intriguing and strangely comforting. As if guessing his
thoughts she turned her head towards him and smiled.

There was a stream in front of them with a narrow steel bridge
and handrail. She stretched her body forward from the waist to
see how far under the bridge she could see. She straightened.

'It's pleasant here.'

He laid an arm casually around her shoulder as if he had done
so a thousand times before.

She grinned. 'Let's have a race.'

It surprised him. She started running across the bridge and
along the lane, he following her. He caught her up at a farm gate
and leaned against it, panting.

'You gained a short head victory.'

She stood there, elbows on the handrail, looking about her.

'Shall we walk some more?'

They did, but silently, through a small wood, following the stream for a little distance before she suggested they go back. He felt he liked it here, it was unpretentious, ordinary, English, but it was the country and lacked buildings, though as they came to the cottage again he could see the attraction of living in such a place.

As she let him in and closed the door she turned, leant against it and smiled. He took her gently by the shoulders and pulled her towards him. He looked at her for a second - a black-and-white filmic hiatus filled by seeing Bogart grab a blonde - and, gripping her harder, kissed her, feeling her teeth thinning her lip. He slowly let go, easing her away from him. She leant against the door again, mouth open in surprise and said, 'Where did that come from?'

'It's what I feel.'

'At this moment?'

'Not just. It's been building for a while.'

She squeezed by him. 'Let's have coffee.'

He followed her into the kitchen, sat at the table and watched her drop spoonfuls of coffee into their cups. She held her mug up to her mouth and, looking over it at him, said, 'Let's slow down, it's a bit too quick for me.'

They finished their drinks without speaking.

'Look, we'll see each other again but... leave it for a little while. I need to start doing something, whatever it is I have to earn a living.'

He took an exaggeratedly resigned breath and asked if she needed any help. She didn't, but thanked him for the offer.

'Social workers get a bad press, I wouldn't like to see you get hurt, the nasty things you may have been able to prevent can't be measured; you can't quantify potential. Anyway, if there's anything I can do.'

She moved towards the front door saying, 'Sorry,' as she opened it.

He stepped out, walked to the gate and turned, but the door had closed. Going towards his car he noticed the long garden at the back of the cottage was part apple orchard with lights coning on under the symmetrically planted trees making them look like enchanted fans. He drove home feeling in abeyance, in an empty no-man's land of emotions unwillingly constrained.

CHAPTER 7

' ... and TV-trained historians and throw their arms about to
emphasise every unfounded statement in a most annoying manner
while looking back on the past in a haze of conjecture, opinion,
second-hand anecdotal misinformation, apocryphal stories, lay
psychology and misplaced nostalgia as a projection of
what they *want* it to be.'

He was listening to Ted where he usually tended to hold court,
at the coffee bar in the foyer of the National Theatre, and who he
saw once a year, if that, and who he'd met when they'd both been
on a pedagogic course in Richmond. He tended to snarl a lot
when delivering opinions, making him rather dislikeable, but
Vincent had kept his occasional company because of the
intellectual stimulus on offer. After a few minutes he bade him
and his cronies goodbye and went to see a film at the nearby Film
Institute.

He was seeing it with Gail. He'd felt frustrated and also
annoyed with himself for what had happened when he'd last seen
her because it had been out of character, and he'd wanted to stay
longer with her. He'd rung her the following day to see if she
wanted to see a movie. She did. He'd asked if she minded the
choice being his. She hadn't.

He met her at the NFT entrance, the restaurant, now under a
recent franchise and without the film posters and LCD's showing
clips of Fellini or Tarkovsky films, appearing a little less
welcoming to cinephiles. He was habitually early, she was late.
Her hair was permed a little; a wide hat pulled forward, a long
skirt, black Cuban- heeled shoes.

'You look like an up-market 'Bisto kid,' he said, assuming
she'd know the reference.

She raised a leg, kicked out a little. 'What am I now, a chorus
girl?'

Her action surprised him; it didn't go with the dated
respectability of her clothes and made her more... carnal; a
reminder perhaps of watching the high-kicking, stocking-clad

theatrical chorus lines of years ago. She seemed different from the first few times she'd been with him, more relaxed, an emotional ponderousness perhaps disappearing. She briefly squeezed his elbow and, inside, listening to the intro by a man whose father had been something like second assistant chief grip best boy on the film, interminably intent on detail and which the boy in Vincent didn't want to hear, wishing to believe that Jane Greer was still twenty three, briefly leant her shoulder against his. It felt warm, pleasant, flirting.

Between watching the *femme fatale's* entrance against the Acapulco sun in 'Out Of The Past,' and her dresses getting darker as she continuously walked out of shadows and into the light, he slyly watched Gail enjoying the film, noticing how small and well-shaped her ears were, one side of her hair pulled back, how smooth her skin. It was an effort to turn back to the screen. They left, talking about what they'd seen, she interested in the photography, clothes, he the mood, the script.

Halfway across Hungerford Bridge - the result of a committee's seduction by Nordic technology - she put her arm inside his, affectionately, without propriety. It was increasingly relaxing to be with her. They found a bar, and between the laughing - her humour alternating between the droll and sharp and interrupted by a lilting laugh - he guessed that this was a woman who was still holding so much in: distress, loss, and who, by long practice, was hiding it. There was also giving there. He wanted to release it, wished her to give it all to him.

It was getting late and as they entered a Tube station the analytic response returned; wanting to know why he was feeling something, experiencing it. This was the child perhaps wanting a mother-Madonna, a glistening, fantasized object; women needing to be, men wanting to have. On the way to the main station they talked again of the film; Mitchum's weary eyes and laconic voice, a violent man wrapped in indifference, the early cutting back to the past. They almost missed their stop.

He went onto the platform with her this time. She squeezed his hand as she stepped onto the train, waved at him through the window as it moved off. He watched the back of the train feeling as if he were in a replay of 'Brief Encounter': the brown carriages, waiting room, porters, steam, the refreshment room tea urn, trilbies, fox furs, the woman, pain in her eyes, brave mouth, travelling away from her almost-lover; the screen in the darkness, the usherettes at the back, torches still, wanting her to run back to him, leap through the smoke, rise above the sooty columns, shatter the roof, soar... Perhaps he'd been watching too many movies.

Knowing he wouldn't sleep much he walked to the bagel shop in Brick Lane again, passing grey-painted gastro pubs with their made-to-order Dalston grot, sporadic bare brick walls, industrial lighting, and furniture the result of raids on junk shops for Victoriana and bargain fifties. He noted the hipsters milling outside them with their Jesus beards, high hair, skinny jeans and pink trainers or long, pointed fifties-style winkle pickers making them look like court jesters, and indulgently quasi-mincing along in their mannered narcissism; the 'young urban professionals' beloved by property developers.

Perhaps tomorrow he would look around an affluent thirties estate or two, maybe Woodford: curved windows, chevrons, coloured glass front doors, steep-pitched roofs and wooden garden gates - a denial of and a bastion against the contrived 'urban 'village,' which they'd never been designed for anyway; more for the professional class and the aspirational clerk and maybe like himself a while ago, the skilled artisan. That barren, impoverished cerebral wilderness of painting and decorating, building sites, hooked to a concrete column hanging over cement floors to bitumen their edges, the 'lick and a promise' jobs in The Bishops Avenue - being given an opened pack of nine cigarettes for a tip - an ex-con threatening to kill him because he'd forgotten to book his overtime in, sacking men, as in telling someone he liked whose employment he was about to end that he had a 'rotten job to do.' 'I'll do it for you Vince,' he'd said enthusiastically, 'what is it?'

And while he was working, painting, paperhanging, organising, on ladders, scaffolds; the unaware escaping from it and himself, at home in his obsessively detailed drawings, making a concrete garden pool complete with pump chamber, fountain and stone waterfall, occasionally working on it till the early hours with a bulb and a lead; trying not to accept what he was doing for a living; his life, the waste.

She had wanted to see him again, but wasn't sure what she felt after he'd kissed her. It had been a long time since someone had done that, not since Stanley. Thinking about it, she felt a sense of something like guilt as if she'd betrayed him, but it wasn't her that had been the instigator, and her husband had gone now. Lying awake she thought about him as she had always known him, a thousand memories, but it was those from the last year that dominated. They saddened her, though she expected them to eventually leave her; the good, the solid, returning.

She was pleased he had rung, she hadn't seen a film in ages, hadn't been anywhere in ages. He'd chosen well, reminding her of how much she enjoyed films, talking about them, sharing them. The demo was, she supposed, a kind of sharing too, but not the funeral, you couldn't share a death, not of someone you'd lived with, who only you really knew.

It had felt easy with him this time, almost as if they were riding a gentle swell, there was no probing, and some enjoyable bits of humour, like his definitions, 'Falsetto - Italian dentures,' and 'A la carte - Muslim wheelbarrow.' She'd tried a few herself till they agreed to stop before they started giggling like a couple of clever school kids. She wondered just how much of the cultural realm she had shared with Stanley; books and films, no, not really, and although he had liked the theatre there hadn't been many stimulating discussions, heated debates; he'd been too equable, even-tempered, more the rational, the economist.

Someone had told him once of a desert island occupied by just three people: an engineer, chemist and an economist with just a tin of beans for food. The engineer had suggested using rocks as a fulcrum to bend the tin open, the chemist suggested leaving it in the sun so that the heated chemicals within would eventually burst the can; the economist had said, 'Assuming we have a tin-opener... ' He'd smiled tolerantly. Maybe she should have added a philosopher who'd asked, 'What tin of beans?'

Vincent seemed to like walking; Stanley hadn't. She'd often walked through the woods even in the winter; there was something about the sight of miles of flat snow covering large tracts of the Island and almost hiding the network of tiny creeks and boardwalks criss-crossing the marshes; and occasionally to the hill where legend had it that the ghosts of two Viking brothers were doomed to fight each night for the love of the same woman.

She didn't like it when seeing people from East London and Essex converge on the place at summer weekends and eat their own bodyweight in oysters, rollmops and prawns before driving back across the Strood; it interrupted her psychological ownership of the Island. Anyhow, she would call him this time.

Vincent had just been treated by his osteopath. He saw him almost annually where he would hear the same tale about his graduation and wearing a t-shirt with 'God made human beings so there would be osteopaths' across it. It was an injury he'd received when, looking out from his Nordic-Brutalist flat on the campus of his sixties plate-glass university, he'd seen a first team trial game which he couldn't help joining. He hadn't played football since youth clubs and when the game had finished he couldn't stand upright. After weeks he could. After years he was told one of his legs was half an inch longer than the other; his left sacrailiac joint having twisted a long time before. It was put back in its natural position in under twenty minutes and when it annually recurred he returned to the same man.

The receptionist had warned him when he'd called that her boss's son had recently died - a skiing accident somewhere - and when he arrived, pressing the bell gently as if to diminish its demanding buzz, the door was opened by her with a dignified slowness.

Coming out Of the treatment room, the osteopath briefly looked at his patient and turned back into it while the latter followed, the former excusing himself briefly while Vincent stripped. When he had previously been there was always the man's chortling laugh pushing into the waiting room, his proud voice speaking of his son's trial for Spurs, hinted at by the school team photo on the wall. His hand was shaken then the usual thumb and finger placed firmly on his hip.

'Leg's long again. Sacrailiac.'

There was no conversation, as if there was an externally created law of silence which neither of them could or wanted to do anything about. His arms in the crux of his patient's he'd pulled him up and around, up and around, but Vincent imagined that in his head he was lifting his child onto his shoulders, podgy legs around his face, and releasing Vincent, the boy helpless with laughter, falls across his bed in the mock fight; kneading his patient's neck, he turns the child's head and sees wide eyes playing hide and seek. As he'd gripped his client's calf, perhaps he saw his lad slide into a tackle or flying up the stairs as his fingers climbed Vincent's spine, and maybe ruffling the boy's hair as his hands dug deeper into the back of his patient's skull.

He left. It had been thirty minutes of emotional limbo; the osteo hardly knowing he was there; he was an object, the leaden stimulus to the automatic response his training and experience dictated. Vincent guessed that it would be months before he began muted, trivial conversations with his patients again.

He wasn't sure why he felt like returning to his childhood street again after so many years, maybe because he'd been with somebody whose child no longer existed, but he caught a bus and walked through the old recreation ground towards it. After a new appreciation of the thirties Tudorbethan public toilet he and his mates had chalked stumps on and played cricket outside, either before or after playing conkers under the numerous chestnut trees, he noticed a basketball pitch in place of the old sandpit and swings with their see-saw escapes from his school's god-fearing Gothic. The bandstand, where the second-rate brass bands with their patched red uniforms played on occasional Sundays, had also disappeared.

He turned along The Portway. Everything, of course, had changed: the old Kinema, the 'Gaff,' had been obliterated by new-builds, Fox's the greengrocers, the fish shop, the garage, even the 'Toby Arms' had gone, though the original fascia of the tobacconist's with its faded, sign-written 'Silburn & Sons' was revealed while the shop was being refitted. It was a vivid mnemonic of his childhood and of his early teens, of Trebor fruit salad, sherbet dips, and persuading the woman behind the counter to sell him a cigarette from a packet of five Woodbines.

Walking slowly, he turned into the street. The pavement trees weren't there then, nor the leaded glass in the Simms' cricket-balled fanlight. He passed Mrs. Burn's, the Thornton's, and then number 27; now stone-dashed and with PVC windows and front door. He didn't stop, just walked on. There was no point, there'd be very little left except the curved wall in the passage, the side door and maybe the outside toilet, now probably used for junk. Maybe one day he would.

There were no slatted blinds and matt front doors then either or, at the end of the road, the Latvian deli as comfortable as a Paris street corner; but opposite, the City Corporation sign at the Park entrance proudly black in the sun was, as well as, barely visible as he peered closely at it, the genitals he'd carved on its edge when he was twelve.

It was getting dark as he continued to the local station, the only welcoming thing being the London Underground's bullseye sticking out from its sooty bricks. He decided to get a bus somewhere. From its upper deck, sitting with, seemingly, a representative speaker of each of London's four hundred and fifty languages and dialects, he could see through the damp twilight the wet chairs outside 'Bob's Café' like a dispirited, doomed attempt to create a *Boulevard San Michelle* bar in Canning Town - a black- and-white photo of the Eiffel Tower just visible on its wall - the tatty but stylish thirties bus garage currently a supermarket, a few grey-leafed trees and a stretch of the Northern Outfall sewer now desperately called 'Greenway.'

Somebody looked up from the pavement, she in her bubble, he in his pondering the futile relativism of everything, and as this statement cannot claim privileged exemption from its own absoluteness is thus self-stultifying and therefore there is no absolute, and if there was, for whom or what would it be an absolute? So, warts and all, it's relativism; there is no meaning. Guided by the imbalance of instincts and society's non-codified laws, people make their own and, in this nihilistic mood, Vincent was incapable of making his.

He sat on the bus as it resumed its return journey, passing the café again, its owner piling up his metal chairs to carry in out of the rain. The lit windows seemed to have a bit of Impressionism about them, Van Gogh, maybe, or Monet, until he decided that they didn't and, in a rare slip into anthropomorphism, that the dark East End evening didn't deserve colour, had done nothing to justify it, wasn't good enough for it. Somehow, the rain suited the night.

Then his mobile rang. It was Gail saying that she was staying with a friend in East London overnight and perhaps he would like to do something the following day. Of course he would. He suggested they go to Greenwich.

'Did you know that the station there is one of five in London that have names with all five vowels in? I know four of 'em.'

This time he wasn't aware that this sliver of trivia was a way of blanketing what he'd begun to feel for her again.

He was early but she soon came along, wearing a red beret that made her grey-green eyes look greener. They had a quick look in the market before wandering around Georgian streets then to the Thames past the Marine College and the cannons on the Walkway.

'Just about my favourite period, Georgian, they built the first terrace, known as 'row houses' and - I'll stop, I sound like an accountant.'

She grinned. 'I love the sun on trees, don't you? I even like chocolate box roses around a front door.'

They walked on, he enthusiastically talking of Italianate towers, scrolled balconies, black-and-white tiled paths, she looking at him, half-smiling as they walked past stone cherubs and leaning gravestones.

'Sometimes,' he said, 'I want to become a roof and look down on porticoes and clicking gates, on gardens, and trees higher than me and, say, an unexpected park, a watercolour lake.'

'Now you don't sound like an accountant,' she said, and then laughed again. 'You're a romantic, Vincent.'

It was the first time she'd used his name. He liked it. He put his arm around her shoulder. She stopped for the briefest moment then put her arm around his waist. They walked on in silence, both feeling the import of their actions.

'When I first came to London I thought that it was all rather grey, the colours absorbed by the streets. There seemed no distance, no sky.'

'What colours do you like?'

'Gold, russet, green.'

'The colours of apples.'

'I suppose they are.'

In an impromptu action she reached across the graveyard railing of the Thames-side church and picked a large petal from a rose, saying with a smile, 'Eat it, it's nice.'

He did, and it was.

After a silence she enthused about the ultramarine dusk, the pink reflections on the water, and asked where he would take her if he wanted a romantic evening. He told her, only half jokingly, that it would be a pie and mash shop. There was one nearby. She enjoyed it. They went back to the river and when the pink reflections turned to the grey-cream splashes of embankment lamps they caught the Light Railway then the Tube back to her station.

There were a lot of people on the concourse, apparently there had been an 'incident' somewhere and trains delayed.

'You're going to have trouble getting back now aren't you. I've the most clichéd suggestion in history, but you could stay at my place.'

She looked doubtful.

'The wait could be hours.'

She nodded.

He took her elbow. 'Come on then.'

On the journey she was quiet, in both train and car.

She admired the glass in his front door, a Japanese Deco design he'd had copied and, inside, he asked if she wanted a drink. No, she was tired. He explained where the bathroom was, and the bedroom. He left her for ten minutes then went up. She was lying in his bed, the duvet over her. He lay next to her. She gently kissed his shoulder before saying goodnight and turning her back.

'It's better to be friends than lovers,' she said quietly.

It seemed to be a mature woman's gambit, the earth mother offering a comforting, 'There, there.' to a little boy. But he felt it was an act; that she wanted more than this.

'What about both? They're not mutually exclusive.'

She seemed a little reluctant at first, but not for long.

He lay there afterwards full, sated. He felt that she was also.

In the morning, after a quick breakfast, the first time in years he'd had company for the meal, she told him she'd arranged to meet a solicitor regarding her husband's estate.

'The will and... you know.' She looked at him firmly. 'I don't want to go.'

'Good, the feeling's mutual.'

'Another time.' she offered with a smile then, moving towards the admired door, she went out onto the pavement. He drove her to the local station, leaving her there, not travelling to the main line one with her, perhaps not wanting to see her get into another train, going away from him again.

Feeling in limbo he drove to his favourite café in Wanstead, noticing at the side, in retro Deco glory, its owner's jade green and ivory Nissan Figaro with its cream leather seats, stylized dashboard, white-walled tyres and boasting a price tag out of the reach of a mortgage-laden lecturer. On the way he'd passed a mosque with its open double doors and a speaker with a twenty decibel call to prayer - wondering what would happen if he stood outside with a megaphone preaching atheism.

Looking idly into a nearby photographic studio he saw a distraught little boy with his parents preparing to have their photos taken. An elderly Chinese man came in wishing everyone loud, good-natured good mornings with repeated 'Herro darlin's' like an oriental Benny Hill and offered the boy a lollipop. His father frowned and told him that if he wanted his child to have confectionery he would buy it himself. Vincent was about to point out to him that the man merely wanted to make his son feel better, when he guessed that his 'would' really meant 'could' and that he'd probably known somewhere a level of poverty which ensured that when he was capable of paying for something he wanted the world to know.

It reminded him of a rather pointless visit to a Chinese herbalist a few years before to see if they had something to ease longstanding stomach pains. The attractive girl, actually wearing a cheongsam, had asked him, 'How many time you go shi'?' and 'Wha' your shi' like? Is hard? Soft? Wha' your shi' like?'

It was cheap amusement, lad-ish humour, but he felt a little lad-ish; felt good. It was a while since he'd been with a woman and he was intrigued by this one, and it was becoming more than that. He didn't have to try to stop analysing himself, because at the moment he wasn't. He simply wanted her with him.

CHAPTER 8

It had been a while since Billy had been to a strip club, only once before had he visited one. Entertainment usually meant being with his mates; a football match, seeing a show up west, the club; but as he had quite a few orders for copies of his photos taken at the latter's last do he had taken the digital versions to a photo shop in Soho to be printed. Walking back along Old Crompton Street past a neon lit 'Girls-Girls-Girls' spread over a large window he had decided to go in.

The bouncers at the entrance were large, the walls and ceilings were red with black tables and chairs, the music quiet but raunchy. There were about fifty men, their drinks being served at the tables by two girls in red looking like an amalgam of bunny girls and air hostesses. It was a kind of mini-theatre in the round.

The performers, two blonde girls in strips of flimsy ribbon, glass-like high heeled shoes and lit by green and blue spotlights, were sensuously sliding up and down poles like snakes around an erection. 'Cabaret' seemed like an age of innocent decadence. He mused on why there were no black girls, which prompted him to think of one he'd known intimately.

He'd met her at the club; rarely did an African go there, especially one who could jive, which she was doing with enthusiasm, a large grin and an imaginary partner. He'd joined her, they'd danced well together. He'd chatted her up and they met in a pub a few days afterwards. She wore a Diana Ross wig and briefly told him about herself: brought up outside Pretoria, she'd managed a restaurant before coming to London and its gold-paved streets.

Thinking she'd like it, he'd taken her to see the Passion play, 'The Mysteries' in which the director had encouraged members of the African cast to act in their own languages. She casually told him she could speak five of them. On the way back he'd mentioned that the lead black singer, the best voice on stage, should have played Eve. She made no comment, just shrugged.

He tried to get her interested in the songs, the humour, the scant, but effective scenery; like the stockade made of giant Peter Stuyvesant cartons in which a near naked group had sung, 'You Are My Sunshine,' and received a standing ovation. She shrugged again then said, 'I will stay with you tonight then.'

She had; whispering afterwards 'I am a wounded soldier making love on the battlefield,' she'd gone to sleep. He hadn't understood what she meant.

He told his friends about her. They'd looked surprised.

'There's an AIDS epidemic in Africa,' George had warned him. 'What's the attraction?' 'Hold 'em upside down they all look the same,' Sid had said, and 'Showing us you're as liberal as the next man are yer?' was another comment from somebody, and George had continued with 'How you gonna feel when two old ladies in a café serve her burnt toast and a dirty mug 'cos they know she's with you?' though he had had a couple of 'You lucky bastard's.'

She'd probably felt his uncertainty early on. He hadn't seen her again, and never did see what was under the wig.

The girls performed vertical splits, left the poles and, after an embrace and a long kiss on each others lips with the audience cheering, they ran off to a side door. The music then changed to something slow and bluesy and, with her black hair and a long, classically cut white dress, the lead girl entered. She turned gradually towards everyone, hands moving down from her neck, undoing buttons slowly and provocatively. She bent forward for the last one, straightened and, with a slight shrug of her shoulders, the dress slipped to the floor. Then the sound of a hybrid of orchestral and military music trumpeted out and, twirling the miniature tassels on her bikini top, she kicked out, shimmied her hips and slowly ran her hands from her breasts to below her thighs and kicked high again.

She put her hands behind her and began to undo her top then, looking coquettishly over her shoulder, decided not to and started to sway around the raised dais, again spinning her tassels. Her purposely retro act seemed more at home on Prohibition era Broadway than in a strip club and with no gallery to play to she became everyone's, even the bunny girls had stopped serving to watch her. She repeated her routine twice more, each time the backward glances more provocative, her bikini top increasingly not quite undone. When she swayed off there were cheers, clapping, whoops and then loud chatter.

He'd like to see Gail do something like this. He imagined her on his bed standing atop his fifties Arondac blue wool blanket kicking off her shoes and putting her hands inside the waist of her jeans.

'You wanna see a strip?' she'd say. 'How's this?'

She would begin exaggeratedly rotating her hips while undoing the buttons of her blouse then slowly pulling it off. Putting her arms behind her she'd loosen her bra, letting it fall on the bed, and stand there legs apart, showing him her breasts almost defiantly. She would undo the button at the waist of her jeans and slowly unzip the fly. Putting her outstretched hands inside them she'd work them down her thighs till they dropped around her feet. She'd kick them away from her then sway her hips again as the fingers of both hands went inside her knickers, saying 'D'you like this baby, d'you like it?'

She would push her forefingers into her crotch then quickly pull them out and holding her drooping hands high above her head, flicking her fingers towards him, she'd whisper 'I'm a viper, I have forked tongue. Ssss …'

That would be really something. As if.

He wondered how she was, it had been a little while since her old man had died, and as she didn't have to go to that home every day now, what was she doing with herself? He'd seen Becky for a little while and she'd mentioned that her pal had been out with someone, though wasn't sure who he was. He didn't like hearing that, but perhaps there was nothing in it, just a friend or something.

He liked people, always had, couldn't help it he supposed, just like he'd always eaten food quickly, wiping around the plate with his finger so as not to waste any. But whoever he was he felt he wouldn't like him. Perhaps when he saw her again he should cut the jokes a bit, perhaps she saw him as a bit loud or something. He'd crept up behind her in Rihad's once and told her a joke.

'There's this Jew and he says to this...' Immediately she'd turned around he knew he should have stopped before the end, but he hadn't. He knew women usually liked him; he'd read somewhere they were attracted to men who made them laugh. Maybe he could tell her a few cleaner ones next time he saw her, though he wasn't sure if he knew any.

It had been a long time since she'd been with anyone; including Stanley. She certainly hadn't been looking for it. She wasn't really sure why she'd gone home with him but realised that she must have wanted him, though after using the black-tiled bathroom she'd felt lost, disoriented. His bedroom was nice though, magnolia with green curtains and some small pre-Raphaelite prints in those distinctive greens and greys, and a sepia one of nude Edwardian women standing and laughing with each other. She lay on the duvet cover feeling strange, yet there was something fresh, too. She slid underneath it. When the bed thumped down soon afterwards she really did just want friendship, but he hadn't. She was glad of it. It had always been with Stanley. She'd missed it.

And it was good; his body was slim and smooth for his age, though she didn't know what that was. He was patient, so controlled, unless he hadn't wanted her as much as she'd thought he had. No, he'd wanted her and she had complied.

It was all good, the walks, talks, the laughs. She'd responded to him in lots of ways, almost not recognising the feelings, and felt kind of creative when with him; a long while since Stanley had made her feel like that. But she was comparing, she musn't, it was pointless, odious. She wouldn't do it again, she would compartmentalise them: one was here, the other dead. She felt tears again. She dabbed her eyes and decided she wouldn't do this any more either.

Vincent was outside a church looking up at its spire. He was waiting for Gail at Camden Lock. He liked churches, but not what went on inside them; still partly the opiate of the masses - only in recent years had that divine legitimation of fatalistic acceptance, 'The rich man in his castle, the poor man at his gate, all creatures high and lowly, god ordered their estate.' been scrapped - but the aesthetics of Norman battlements, of spires, leaded glass windows, flying buttresses, a church smell of peaceful calm - though secretly thinking that municipal cleaners used aerosols labelled 'church smell,' 'museum odour' and the like.

She was punctual, and with a slightly mocking smile said, 'Have I smashed a stereotype? I even worked out where the south side of the High Street was.'

'A slight crack. And there are reasons why females are no good at spatial concepts; that's why I rarely ask women for directions.'

'I know where this is going and you'll lose, but I'd like to see the market.'

As they walked past the canal-side café where the narrow boats were moored he asked if she wished to go in. She reiterated her desire for the market. They went across to it. She was like a gentle throwback in the centre of a circle of the young, with their pierced noses, dyed hair and striped stockings. She bought a filigree brooch, hand mirror, a pair of dressmakers scissors then suggested they eat.

They went back to the café. Just before they sat at a table she saw something which made her laugh. It was a sound that seemed to light the room, like the sun that suddenly illuminated the bridge and the train crossing over the canal. As he ordered he noticed the music, alien at first, then he was back at the 'Palais' - ballroom taught them by a teacher at Tech - leaning on a wall wearing a retro draped jacket, Tony Curtis hair and hearing his mates, 'ere, she might let yer 'ave a bit o' tit.' He watched the 'Jenny Wren' tying up and thought back to the market: Goths gear, rockers, punks, the past …

'Are you still with me?'

He apologised. He was doing this increasingly; wandering back to early years. It seemed obvious that her comparable times were an emotional and cultural remove from the experiences that had formed him.

'I'm hungry,' she said, 'let's have lunch here, unless it's too greasy spoon for you.'

He told her it wasn't, but thought it may be for her.

'Oh, contraire, I love stodge and fry-ups.'

He perversely liked her for this; he, having partly reconstructed himself years before and, at least symbolically, moving away from that culinary environment, and her defying conditioned taste buds and shifting towards it.

They ate their meal, He let her do the talking, finding out more about her, her late parents, her house, childhood things, the urge, the need, to do something for a living, but nothing about her late husband.

Before she had to go back they enjoyably used a few hours with a boat trip to Little Venice then walking to the café on the bridge over the canal tunnel. She was talkative, animated, and there was a quiet sense of an emotional security that she probably wasn't aware of; people who were rarely recognised it, it informed the world they saw. He was envious.

As they walked he was even more intrigued by her, not least by the hat she wore, the jacket, the ruffle shoulder pads of her blouse, and the way she walked, as if steel tips on her heels would have made no sound. And her laugh, coming from a bright, loved, honest place that he wanted to know, would have liked to share.

Looking down on the canal, he mentioned that this little piece of London reminded him of Norwich, where he'd been a student and whose river valley had now been turned into a lake for the richer students to sail their yachts on. She asked him if he'd been back there. He told her he was there the previous year when he'd returned to read some of his poetry in the English Faculty.

'I read poetry, don't write it.'

'You can be my groupie next time.'

'You're on,' she said, raising her glass of tea as if it was wine.

He walked to the Tube with her then on to the mainline station. He asked if she would change her mind and stay with him the night. As if expecting the question she replied quickly, 'No, things to do. But soon; promise.'

She kissed him at the barrier, walked along the platform and into a carriage.

On the way back, holding a rolled newspaper in front of him like a dagger to ward off somebody's backpack pushing nearer as the train grew more crowded - the man eventually glowering at him while he removed it - an image conjured itself of her walking down the canal steps in front of him: her hand bent out, fingertips sporadically touching the handrail, her high heels on each step at the same angle of descent, shoulders moving smoothly down, her bag swinging like a pendulum.

Some time after arriving home she rang to invite him over for the following evening. He accepted gladly.

He left after dinner - his culinary expertise limited mostly to toad-in-the hole, shepherds pie and warming up local take-aways - and had been driving for just a few minutes when, as he stopped at traffic lights, he was startled by an aggressive fist hammering on his side window. He wound it down and saw a large face, eyes bulging.

'You hit my car, you know you bastardwell did.'

He remembered that about a mile back there'd been a car parked opposite a traffic island. He'd slowed down to pass.

'Did I? I didn't feel - '

He hadn't noticed the jack handle the man was holding. He pushed the sharp end into the side of Vincent's neck, the latter deciding instantly to treat him as if he was an angry, potentially violent workman on a site where he was a foreman. Looking into his eyes he calmly told him to take the tool away from his throat. He did, slowly.

Vincent pointed out that as the lights were now green he was going to turn left into the main road and stop. He suggested the man follow him and they'd talk. He drove round the corner, got out of the car, stepped onto the edge of the pavement and stood against the guard rail. His attacker climbed out of his vehicle with another, shorter man.

They came towards him. He repeated that he hadn't known he'd hit the car. The smaller one said, 'Look, mate, 'e's my bruvver, his wife's taken his kid and gone. 'e's in pain.'

'Yeh, I'm sorry mate,' said the one still holding the lever, 'he's right, I'm 'urtin', I really am, but you'll have to pay for the damage.'

Vincent walked around to the side of the car. There was a long scratch on the driver's door. Acting as rationally as he could, he asked its owner how much he thought it would cost. He told him; it sounded reasonable. He knew he had a cheque with him, a rare occurrence, wrote it and handed it over. They then heard the quick burst of a siren and a police car pulled in front of them. They were like a stationary mini convoy now. Two constables stepped out; one with a tube with a lump on the end which Vincent guessed was a breathalyzer.

'Anything wrong, sir?' the officer asked, looking directly at him.

Surprisingly, jack man said, 'No, it's okay, we're just having a chat, haven't seen each other for a while.'

Still looking at Vincent the constable said, 'Sure you haven't been drinking, sir?'

Vincent told him he'd had a couple of glasses of wine. That it was a breathalyzer was confirmed by its use.

'It's right on the line sir, I can charge you or not.'

Putting an arm around Vincent's shoulder, his previous assailant said, 'Oh, come on, it's a lovely sunny day, the birds are coughin', you're not gonna nab him for one drink are yer?'

The officer looked at the three of them, nodded and got back in the car with his colleague and drove off. After the two brothers had bizarrely told Vincent to ''ave a good one,' he continued his journey.

An hour later, leaning against the inside of Gail's cottage door, he breathed a deep sigh of relief and stood there while she stood in front of him asking if he was alright. He told her what had happened. She squeezed his arm.

'Perhaps god protected you.'

He moved away. 'What's this then, the idea that the Lord has rewarded my, or rather your, faith or that his favours are pre-destined' - he'd stepped away from the door, arms out, hands offering the mordant choices - 'or was it written in the stars?'

Realising his irritation was partly due to delayed shock; he took a deep breath and let it out slowly, in little pieces.

'I'm sorry, forgive the sarcasm.'

'It's alright. Have a drink with me.'

He did, and several more before they went to bed. Later, he lay there thinking as she slept quietly and deeply at his side, that she had done little more than taken him into her, more or less obeying a biological response, a duty, without any obvious enjoyment. He wondered if she was purposely providing a comfort, a salve for the car incident.

In the morning they did some more walking, similar territory as before but deeper into the woods, she repeatedly looking around at the trees, grass, the bushes, seemingly knowing the names of everything growing and pointed out some spots where she'd camped as a child. They found a pub and after smoked-mackerel pâté, fishcakes and scallops washed down with a bottle of Mersea Mehalah, a dry local wine, he felt better, dismissing his previous doubts and wondering whether she would want him to again stay the night.

On the way back to her house they were almost out of the trees when he remembered that he'd arranged with his publisher some weeks previously that he would read for him that evening; it was his last event before selling the business which he'd started and kept flourishing for ten years. She asked him where it was.

'Can I come with you? I'm seeing a man I need to see about,' she paused, 'the estate, as they call it. I can still come, his office is near there I think. Can anybody read? It's called open mike isn't it?'

'Yes, why?'

'Just wondered.'

He'd like her there; maybe he could impress her a little, too. They went back together in his car, he dropping her off near her solicitor's while he went to the venue.

It was in 'The Basement,' a Covent Garden poetry venue where his collection had been launched two years previously; he had the last guest spot. There were fifty people there, leaving just a few empty chairs. As he settled on a sofa at the side of the mini-stage, Gail walked through the curtains at the bottom of the stairs. He thought she would arrive later. Huddled and tip-toeing she went towards the back of the room, catching Vincent's eye and smiling.

After one of the guest poets had finished - a grey-haired man with a black homburg hat and matching cape whose self-indulgent attempts to match sound effects to the narratives of his poems were increasingly annoying an impatient audience - those who had put their names down for the open mike spots began to read: younger ones either full of bright-eyed enthusiasm or an almost shaking shyness, and a couple of older hands who read as well as they crafted their work. At the interval he beckoned to her and they went upstairs for a glass of wine and to chat with a poet he knew from other venues, introducing Gail. When he'd finished he asked her what she thought so far.

'Interesting, I think it's like I thought it'd be, I'm not sure.'

Downstairs again, the compere ushering on more readers, Vincent sat back in his chair and heard Gail's name called. For a second he wasn't sure what was happening then she stood and walked rather shyly to the little stage. She had removed her coat, revealing a red pleated frock with shoulder pads and a belt with a black bow.

She looked taller under the lights and her voice was stronger than he had expected it to be, clear and, in certain passages from her work, lyrical. She didn't look at her poems much, just the occasional glance. He knew she read poetry, but not that she wrote it. Speaking of metaphor moons, of cliffs, clouds and cormorants, she spiritualized salmon, eulogised larks, yet as her foot tapped to the meter, her groin subtly pushing forward, slightly gyrating, she turned her sentimentalised, neo-Victorianism into the body, into skin and breath and touch, into the visceral just by her bodily movements. There was a contained waywardness about her, an almost disingenuous sexuality; the difference between the contents of her poems and the effect almost dichotomous.

The audience didn't clap between her poems as, sometimes reluctantly and politely, they had done with the other poets. They were quiet. She stepped from the stage and was halfway to her seat before the clapping began and which seemed louder than for most of the previous readers. Vincent looked again to where she was sitting, looking down as if she'd shrunk inside of herself - though, for him, the way she sat, her knees resting against each other, hands in her lap, still holding her poems, her sensuality hadn't diminished.

It was his turn. His head was full of her, but he couldn't just stand behind the mike and mumble. He didn't really want to read, he had no new work; and though he had a few copies of his collection with him to sell to anyone interested, if they weren't he wouldn't bother to persuade them. A reviewer had written of the 'remarkable clarity' of his work. He knew it thoroughly, had overworked it; felt that 'remarkably dull' was more appropriate. He took a deep breath, vowed as usual to lose the glottal stoppage, and began.

He knew the poems that worked, where he'd get a laugh, a frown of interest, appreciative nods. He read his favourites: the boyhood ones, the New York, the Prague ones and his well-read surreal piss-take on over-figurative poets. He could just see her at the back of the room; she was still looking at her lap. When he finished, almost forgetting to make his intended short speech of thanks to Len, his now ex-publisher who was inviting everyone to join him upstairs for free drinks, he felt disappointed, like an adolescent who had tried to impress, had shown off to an attractive girl and who hadn't noticed. He went to her as she was putting on her coat.

'I don't know what to say.'

'I wanted to surprise you.'

'You certainly did.'

'Was I okay?'

'How did the meeting go? Not too upsetting?'

'What did you think of my poetry? Did I read it adequately? I used to write it as a child and, though I'd forgotten, as a teenager, guess it's part of adolescence, but since you mentioned you wrote it I found the old ones and started writing a few new ones.'

'Some are good, I'm glad you wrote them, I'd like to see them, difficult to judge when they're being read. Poets, like Victorian children, should be seen and not heard I think, except you of course.'

After brief goodbyes to Len and a few others, he suggested a quick drink somewhere before she went back. In a nearby pub, a typical London gastro one with cleaned-up Victorian bricks, the fascia and windows painted dark matt grey, potted plants by the entrance and, inside, a terra cotta dining area, they discussed the evening for a while then heard himself say, to push away the fear of rejection, 'The head of UKIP said recently that he'd spent twenty years 'building the brand.' How's that for an example of the dominion of corporate-speak, of politics being just another part of globalised … ' He asked her again if she would come back to his home with him. She thought for a moment and said 'Yes.'

He could see them talking at the bar, he hadn't at first noticed them from his table. He was surprised at seeing her there. He wondered who the bloke was. Not wanting to see the late show at the club, he'd gone to Covent Garden - much changed since his dad had worked there as a porter in the old market - to see if the pub he used to take him to was still there.

He didn't want her having conversations with this man, being with him, listening to him. And she looked so good in her forties gear; the cute shoulder pads, that dress; she was probably wearing it for him, though he would have liked her in fifties stuff, she'd look great in a bolero jacket and flared skirt, he'd tried before to get her to wear something like that but she wouldn't.

She was listening to the man avidly; she had that look that seemed to indicate that she'd listen like that whatever he was saying. Perhaps he was smart, had the gab; but he was pretty smart himself really. She looked across at him for a second then back again. She wasn't going to beckon him over and introduce him. She was his friend; she didn't seem to want to know now.

He stood and walked across to them, standing behind her; which he seemed to be doing most times he saw her.

'Hello Gail.' He turned to her friend. 'Hello mate.'

The latter nodded. Billy looked straight at him and said, 'Knock knock.'

Her friend sighed. 'Who's there?'

'To.'

'To who?'

'No,' said Billy, 'to *whom*.'

'Amusing,' said the man. 'Do I know you? Does Gail?'

'We're old friends aren't we,' he grinned, looking at her.

'Yes, I suppose so.'

'How's things then, alright? Not your usual territory is it.'

'Perhaps not. Look, Billy, I've to get back tonight, we were about to go anyway.'

She smiled at her companion.

'Yes, that's us,' he said.

The man helped her on with her coat and they simultaneously nodded at him as they turned away and went out of the pub. So this was the bloke Becky had mentioned. He didn't like what he was feeling.

This was the second time she'd been asked to his house. Previous to the first occasion the last time she'd been invited, alone, to a man's home had been Stanley's when she'd first known him and he'd rented a small flat near his parents. She hadn't given it much thought, but here it was more suburban than she'd expected: crab pear trees and birches on the pavements, some evergreens and trimmed privets - the number of these obviously decreasing with run-ins and residents preferring close-up views of backsides of cars from front windows. His were curved, while everything inside seemed white and green with paintings of large butterflies on the staircase wall and a neatly contained mural in the through-lounge along with framed sketches which, she assumed, he had done. Such detail; her own work was broader, more colourful, abstract rather than representational and was quickly worked.

There was a minimum of furniture, it was all tidy, organised and with, maybe, something lacking. While she looked around the place at his invitation, he rather fussily offered the usual beverages and suggested they could, if she liked, go out for a meal instead of her suffering his cooking.

The place was nearby and as they sat amongst white loom chairs and tiffany lamps watching a waitress outside carrying rubbish, appearing and disappearing like Morse code as she passed the side windows, she was guessing she was Polish and probably fluent in at least one other language, unlike herself, being able to merely mimic them a little. She thought of the old joke. 'What d'you call someone who speaks two languages? Bilingual. Who speaks four or more? Multi-lingual. Someone who speaks one language? English.'

She briefly felt linguistically inadequate and chose her food.

They enjoyed their meal together and went back to Chisholm Road.

He tried to remember when someone had last shared his bed; it was probably Nyla. It didn't matter. Gail was here now. This time as she slept, he quietly got out of bed, went to his office in the next room and tried scribbling a poem about her, or rather the images he had of her, although when he'd finished and remembered some of the lines from her work; the doves, blossom, sunsets, the lambs, he smiled at the ludicrous difference between what she'd actually read and the almost lustful sensibility he'd picked up from her.

After breakfast - he was so used to eating this alone that for a brief moment a ritualised part of him felt uncomfortable that she was sharing it with him - he asked her if she liked football, his local team were playing and a steward friend had given him some spare tickets. He hadn't thought about using them, though when she answered that she'd seen a few games in the past, he was pleasantly surprised and asked her to come.

It was stimulating to see her in a new environment with bustling crowds around them. She was caught in the feel of the game, knew the names of a few players and, tongue-in-cheek, joined in the orchestrated riposte when the home team levelled the score, of 'You're not fuckin' larfin' now.' She asked him if he minded her swearing. 'It's the only time I do, I suppose.' He didn't. She even ate the obligatory half-time pie.

On the way out of the stadium, shielding her from the crush, he felt she was getting inside of him now, becoming a part of him, a large, fascinating, increasingly deeper segment.

'There's a Japanese film on at that cinema we passed. Want to see it? she asked.

Usually after a match he'd go home thinking of the game; a film seemed too separate an experience to assimilate comfortably, but he felt he would have gone anywhere with her, even shopping.

It was a contemporary silent film about Tokyo which they talked about effortlessly for over an hour on the way back to his place. It was all so easy and joyful. They laughed and mimicked, satirised, childishly, adolescently. They were being ridiculous; the hyperbole, the laughter, the mood continuing through the night. They didn't make love till dawn lightened the curtains.

The next night it was her place again. While she was cooking a meal he looked around her home once more and, with her permission, more comprehensively. It was Victorian but enjoyable, not oppressive like his early experiences, his parents doggedly sticking to the aesthetics of the period in which the house was built. The 'winged victory' bronze on the mantle piece over a Zebo-blacked range stove, the dark spindle struts of the banister rail, brass stair rods, and their bedroom with the mahogany wardrobe and chest where he'd once seen a packet of 'Ona' contraceptives inside a partly open drawer, still evoked a heavy, claustrophobic grimness - the smell of lavender furniture polish filling him with an olfactory repugnance even now - that would drape over his spirit like a tarpaulin. Yet here in this place, he saw, felt, sometimes similar objects and shapes differently. There was a sort of delicate artfulness about them, a Pre-Raphaelite depth, an intrigue, a feel of her, of fun.

That night they began playing out an almost exhausting joyousness of sexual scenarios which continued at his place the next night then at her cottage a few days later, then in his home again. He was the wartime American pilot over here picking up a debutante, an East End spiv seducing a waitress, a monsignor claiming his rights; occasionally the quick aside from the impromptu scripts where he'd tell her how convincing that accent was, that glance; the quick scribbling of 'Rape!' on a torn sheet of paper and she throwing it out the bedroom window and her coming back to herself worrying that somebody just might find it.

They'd drink a little, though not much, but it was exciting, adventurous, and so unexpected. She didn't know she was capable of doing it: their little plays, sketches, scenes. He'd wanted her to be a young boy's aunt who'd caught him playing with himself and her taking him in hand, literally, then he suggested he be a Lord and she a scullery maid working in the big house - they'd even fixed some broom and paint roller handles to the bed corners as posts.

It was she who had the idea of him being a milkman successfully chatting up a housewife. It was also an excuse for wearing some of her increasing period wardrobe. She was a land girl again with her hair in a bun and overalls which she'd found in the garage. She knew they were Stanley's, but it didn't matter. Vincent had worn an old leather jacket and used his American accent for a G.I. though she was unsure of what part of that country he was supposed to be from, but he was pretty good as the milkman, albeit she did draw the line when he suggested he be the Pope and she a choir girl.

In turns, that summer, her bedroom then his became an everywhere.

CHAPTER 9

Vincent had just finished a phone conversation with an 'Andy' who worked for an insurance company, though not before he had to listen to a 'we operate a real-time life environment' message preceded by 'we are experiencing high-call volume' - wondering what was wrong with 'we have a lot of callers waiting' - who asked if his name was spelt with a 'haitch.'

'It's 'aitch,'' he said.

'Right,'haitch.''

'No, there's no 'aitch' in 'aitch,' he responded in a friendly manner.

'It's haitch,' innit, 'haitch,' the man said, sounding rather like the 'rough' working class of sixty years ago trying to be posh.

He had work to do preparing for the beginning of the academic year, willingly interrupting it again by sending an email objecting to the local council's plans to destroy a local High Street landmark, even though it was sixties brutalism, to build another addition to the bling and toxicity of London's skyline - a thirty eight storey tower block to, 'reinvigorate the local economy for this rich and diverse community.' Why, he wondered, were diverse communities always 'rich?'

He'd stated, after his aesthetic objections against a looming, bullying, incongruent construction - 'congruence,' he suspected, not included in the vocabulary of contemporary architectural practice - that the council should be developing the many brown sites the area contained and, possibly invalidating his protest, that the building was largely about the council wanting the rest of East London's boroughs to know that it had a bigger penis than them.

Turning off the radio, with voices repeatedly containing 'issue,' as if 'problem,' 'concern' or 'matter' hadn't been invented, he left work-related things and went to a venue in Hackney to read some of his poems, being rather surprised to have been asked.

It was yet another up-and-coming East London 'events' café. On one side was a pub covered in silver graffiti, on the other a

Victorian biscuit factory being converted to apartments trendily called 'The Biscuit Factory' and surrounded by sixties flats and a run-down nineteenth century industrial estate. The ex-warehouse had a bar with goodies on the side like 'hemp seed rye bread with pecan cheese' and contained bearded twenty-somethings with flat caps and sneakers, and women with Alice in Wonderland tresses.

The host had told him that the drinkers would have to listen because 'they had no choice.' They did, and they exercised it. He excused himself and left, thinking of recently reading that 'writing a book of poetry is like throwing a rose petal into the Grand Canyon and waiting for its echo.'

Gail was busy beginning a counselling refresher course in Colchester and he missed her; missed her being near him, not just carnally, but talking, laughing, being ironic; her sometimes surreal hyperbole matching his. He missed her at his side in his bed; he slept easier then, his sleep less troubled.

During a restless night he'd dreamt of being with an actor whose accent and brutal East End personae - a profile close-up of him saying, 'You c**t,' epitomising English film realism - he despised. Vincent was listening to his gruff, but jocular and surprisingly caring voice in the parlour of his childhood home. Then they were on a street with their arms lightly around each other's waist. They were both laughing. When Vincent pointed out that it wasn't the usual thing blokes did, his companion, touching his hand, told him that when they got there, there would be sex. Though not knowing with whom or where, he felt a pleasing anticipation. Even before he was fully awake he knew the actor symbolised his father.

He'd thought of him the previous evening, trying again to understand, to forgive, and had an image of him not as the alien figure he'd had to live with, but as a weak, unhappy victim of his own father's physical abuse, and someone who, frightened of his son's early brightness, had blotted out any wish to understand his offspring. Vincent had said almost aloud, 'I forgive you.' before the obscuration came clouding in again.

The actor had become a generic parent, one he'd wanted to laugh with, to be touched by. Perhaps, for the lost child, the wish for a different father was a beginning of homoeroticism, of, perhaps, homosexuality. He had woken from his drowsy analysis thinking, 'I don't *want* to be fucked by Ray Winstone.'

He went to work, Yolande, one of the mature students, coming in late as usual - this time, it being an Africa Cup year, swinging her hips in a yellow and green Cameroonian football shirt - while Patience, one of the older women, frowned at him while his eyes unavoidably followed her sister African to her seat. Matronly Patience had transferred from a day class because, as she'd whispered tearfully to him in an empty staffroom the previous term, one of the female students had called her, unjustifiably, a 'prostitute'; the ultimate African slur. She had then asked him to come to a church with her and listen to her testimony. Intrigued at what this may be and as he hadn't attended church since a child other than a few marriages and funerals, he'd gone.

It was a Victorian building whose builders would never have envisaged the nature of this congregation. There were many people present, mostly ethnics, the majority Africans. The pastor, white, tanned, grey hair, tailored sports jacket, briefly shook his hand.

'Hi, I'm David,' he drawled in an American accent, and moved into the hall.

'Hi, I'm a sceptic,' Vincent said under his breath as he climbed to the back of the balcony.

He stood watching the keyboard player hitting the chords with a gospel band and, pointing to the hymn-filled screen above the stage and telling them that this was their god for the morning, the pastor led the congregation into their devotional karaoke. Matrons sang, clapped and swayed, and towards the far side of the balcony he saw two students he'd taught the previous year looking across at him, eyes wide in surprise. He exaggeratedly raised his shoulders and gestured with open hands to them.

Patience arrived late, African time, shook his hand and introduced him to her partner who was a pleasant looking Ghanaian who welcomed her teacher warmly and asked him to sit with them. Vincent politely declined and stayed where he was. After an evangelising sermon, the energy of which he hadn't experienced before, and further hymns it was time for her testimony.

Standing in front of the congregation she told them how she had come to god. She recited it very quickly and emotionally and he could understand little. After she had finished, with more clapping and singing from the now packed church, she came up to the balcony and gently squeezed his arm and asked him if he would take her back to his home so she could tell him what had really happened.

Sitting at his dining table with him, she'd held his hands tightly together as if he were praying and, with her eyes closed, told him that when she was nineteen her ancestors had occupied her spirit and told her to remain chaste and that when it was time for her to work for them she would be told. She assumed that, like chosen others in her country; she would need to 'go away' for a few years then return as a healer.

Apparently, the ancestral spirits had recently returned - in what form she didn't say - and demanded that she walk into the sea and there would be a crocodile waiting for her with open mouth into which she would climb. There would be snakes, a festive party and great happiness inside the creature. There she was to stay until ready to heal the sick.

As she told him this she spoke rapidly, became excited; several times he gently slowed her down. She became more agitated, almost frantic, when she announced that she had, wearing white knickers and white dressing gown, set out to obey these wishes three weeks previously at Southend-on-Sea while her younger sister and her boyfriend had watched from the beach.

Resisting explaining the phallic symbolism of the snakes, he imagined her, oblivious to the sounds of boy racers, the pier train, fun fair, go-karts, the smell of vinegar and chips, moving deeper and deeper into the sea. Part of him wanted to laugh out loud at the sheer incongruity of the town she'd chosen, but he believed her; believed her when she told him that as her head was going under water, god had exploded inside of her and told her to renounce what she was doing and to do His work, and only His.

She had waded back to her sister and pleaded with her to find a priest. They'd driven back and found the church - the one she had been speaking in an hour before - and she had told David what had happened. This had been her first visit since then.

She began to cry. Releasing his hands he gripped hers. She opened her eyes; they shone with excitement. This was a different reality for him, a spiritual universe he couldn't enter and didn't wish to. He wanted to tell her that many frigid women who gave themselves to Jesus could do so in the knowledge that they didn't have to make love to him. She would, her humour and patience jettisoned, have cried out that it was profane, an insult. She wasn't in the classroom; he wasn't teaching her.

He'd held her tightly for a long while before she left. When she had he wasn't sure why, knowing his secular position, she had told it to him at all. Back in the classroom there had been no acknowledgement from her that she had ever spoken about these things to him.

He would have liked Gail to turn to him, confess things; share things she'd done in her life, and with her husband, though he knew he would have to battle his jealousy for both their sakes.

At the end of the first week of term - a time in which they had long conversations by phone but not seeing each other, she with coursework and still involved in dealing with the will - he was finishing theory with a quick round-up of postmodern meta-narrative, which implied self-stultifyingly that there is no such thing as a meta-narrative, when a student raised his hand asking why postmodernism was such a small part of the syllabus.

'I've just given you one reason. Why d'you ask?'

'Well, I wondered if you favoured Marxism, because postmodernism would invalidate that and - '

'Thus if I were, you thought I might be getting my own back?'

'Yes, I suppose so.'

'Well, any proponent of an established, overarching sociological theory, including right-wing ones, would dislike a scattered string of opinion and conjecture that emphasises an individualistic subjectivity and denies social class and... Do you know any Marxists then?'

He didn't, nor did Vincent, though he had known an anarchist who'd gone on innumerable demos against the State, the 'system.' One day he'd come into their local café with plasters on head and cheeks, and bruised arms he'd suffered from the 'filth's' batons in an alley off Trafalgar Square. For him, the primary function of the police was to protect the interests of the propertied class from attacks by the property-less masses. Vincent had felt rather morally inadequate in comparison. The same student asked why people seemed to know about Marx, even if they weren't sure of or understood his theories.

Vincent told them it was partly bourgeois accommodationism: to ensure that the name of the founder of revolution's modern incarnation and his views became merely a subject to be studied and therefore absorbed harmlessly into the wider culture. Another, usually quiet pupil, asked why Freud's name was also so recognisable.

'Anybody else wonder why apprentice plumbers, Mexican peons, rhubarb growers and sagger makers bottom knockers have all heard of Freud then?' Vincent asked.

They weren't sure. He suggested that, assisted by the media and its control of the dissemination of ideas - 'Those who own the means of material production control the means of mental production' - the ruling class had thrown its weight behind his theories to further its own interests.

'In short, if the world perceives its troubles, its violence, its pathology as a result of the unconscious, attention is then taken away from a critique of its major capitalist institutions. Okay, so it's a little simplistic perhaps, but nevertheless valid.'

He invariably got a buzz from this group and as he left the room after them he was feeling full of purposeless energy, similar to taking the occasional evening class where afterwards, the adrenalin high, it took him a while to get to sleep.

Leaving the college, the feeling moved to a different energy, a fuller, better one as he thought of Gail. It was so right when with her; something he felt should be so. It was deserved, earned by its years of absence, of experiencing nothing like it, at any time, with any one. The other night, again, they had talked and laughed for hours before they'd made love. It was as if they knew something that nobody else understood.

Billy was feeling a bit better. He'd been thinking back, he'd had his share of women, 'course he had. There was Sally, cuddly, saucy, funny; he'd liked her a lot, and Vasilisa the Russian girl he'd met in the other club place, but although he proudly knew a few Ruskie words, *prevyet, dah, niet pozhaluysta, spasibo, poka,* the language problem had been too big, really. He'd like to settle down he supposed, middle-age was creeping up. Chance would be a fine thing though. Perhaps it was him, maybe he should take things more seriously, be a bit more earnest. Wasn't there a play or something about the importance of it? They weren't the be-all-and-end-all though; he had his interests; his camera, music, his clothes.

They'd started a quiz night at the club a few months ago and he was hoping the new bloke would keep it going. His problem was, not what he didn't know but being unable to resist telling people not in his team what he did know. He wasn't so bad now, but they were always bollocking him for saying, sometimes shouting the answers, he couldn't seem to help himself. Like the last time when the question was, 'Who played lead guitar on 'Rock Around The Clock'?' He had to bite his lip to stop himself from declaiming loudly, 'The Comets lead guitarist was Franny Beecher, but on the original recording it was Danny Cedrone,' or in answer to, 'Who did the singer Jett Powers become?' instead of whispering 'J.T. Proby' to George to write down, he said it aloud.

He could sing a bit; the old ones like, 'The Good Life,' and, 'Stranger In Paradise.' He sounded like Tony Bennett, too, he could get the tone just right, but he hadn't played his guitar for some time, needed to practice, really.

He was humming one of Bennett's numbers to himself as he stood around in the local football club's shop waiting for a guided tour of the stadium to begin. It wasn't the Nou Camp or the Bernabeu, but his dad had first bought him here when he was six and neither of them had ever looked around it properly; he'd have liked him to have been here. He looked at the press and media boxes, the function rooms, teams' changing rooms - the well-used management strategy of creating an unwelcoming away team's room with the home club's logo writ large all over it, not enough shower cubicles, cracked tiles and loose clothes pegs were in evidence, as were, in the home dressing room, the numbered shirts of him and his father's heroes.

CHAPTER NINE

Along a corridor were photos of the players of his childhood, amongst them an England amateur centre-forward who, after his playing career had ended, went into teaching and landed up at Billy's old junior school where, as an eleven year old, the latter had played goalie and, inadvertently building up scar tissue on his elbows, used to dive about on the asphalt playground. The ex-sportsman had watched for a while then said to him, 'You are a brave boy, Raines, a very brave boy.' It was, amongst some unpleasant school memories, a pleasant one.

He loved the smell of the game, and the cinder pitches, flooded grass, mud-caked ball, the sound of the ref's whistle piercing his ears, even with dad shouting at him to dive at the feet of opposing forwards as legs like giant slugs marched towards his goal. These were the days when he and his mates, when walking to the ground from the station, used to sing, 'When we walk along the Mile End Road, doors and windows open wide, when we see a bobby come, up with the ball and away we run, we are the Stepney boys.'

He left the place, turning to look at the mock, cream-painted castles at the sides of the main entrance half expecting to see Mickey Mouse skip out of this tiny Disneyland and give the fans a hug. Turning into the main road and noticing the statue of the Club's players who had once 'won' the World Cup, he passed a pie and mash shop which had, on match days, the longest queues of any such place in the city. He then went into a shop where he would occasionally browse, hoping to find some fifties magazines with Vogue fashion styles - he had a crate of them at home - or some ties. He'd got some of his best ones there: a Ricky, a Cohama California swagger, a Tootal and an Esquire cravat.

Fancying a sit down in the quiet of Rihad's, he caught a bus. Becky was leaving as he entered. He asked after her friend, she told him they'd both be in there tomorrow. He decided he would, too.

Not knowing what time they would be there - he should have asked - he went at midday and over-ate for an hour while listening and talking to an expat South African telling him of the old-fashioned tribal remedy for AIDS - and which apparently President Zuma had taken - which was to have sex with a baby of either gender. Billy attempted to lighten the conversation with a joke.

'I didn't know Mugabe was born in Yorkshire till I spoke his name backwards.'

The man liked it, said he'd put it on social media, shook hands and went. Gail arrived soon afterwards.

She seemed surprised to see him. He told her that her friend said she would be here.

'Been waiting for you for about two hours, I have.'

'Didn't ask you to.'

'I know, but I wanted to see yer. That's a kind of wartime boiler suit you've got on an' it?'

'Yes, Becky likes me to wear this sort of stuff. And I do too. I think you know that.'

'You look good. Getting over it, uh? I wanted to ask you who the geez in the pub was when I last saw you.'

'I don't think that's any of your business really, Billy. He's a... friend.'

'I don't wanna upset yer, just wondered that's all. Clever bloke is he?'

'Why do you ask that?'

'Well, something about him I suppose, got that sort of air about him, that persona. So are you of course, clever, I respect that. What's he do?'

'Paints; draws a bit.'

'No, for a living.'

'He works at a college.'

'Got stuff in common then.'

'Yes.'

'Talk about art a lot, do you?'

'Sometimes.'

'What's he think of your place?'

'What makes you think he's been there?'

'Trick question, really. A big word man is he? Just talk, do you? We can discuss photography if you like, that can be an art form you know: focus, stops, speeds, depth-of-field, coloured filters, portraiture, action, etcetera, it's all there. I won a competition once. I took a shot of this baby crawling and put him in a shot I'd taken early one Sunday up west and put him in it so he's crawling around the corner of Regent Street, even had a hand on top of some traffic lights he did. 'Surreal' they called it. You don't do that in your work, do yer, it's all about painting haphazardly annit? though they are bright and I liked the one with the striped deckchair under a palm tree on the beach.'

Just then Becky came in, paused, turned around again as her pal got up and said, 'Let's go. Bye.' though the last could have been fot Rihad who'd just come down the stairs, she'd looked at no-one.

Billy pulled open the door and said loudly to the disappearing backs of the two women, 'Enjoy your intellectual chats with your man friend then Gail, enjoy the art, and I bet that's not the only thing you're enjoying.' He went back in again.

'Everything alright?' asked Rihad.

'No, not really, mate. I'm goin'.'

He went out and started walking the opposite way, feeling snubbed, rejected and, after a while, wondering why she made him feel this way. He supposed it was partly because he'd got his hopes up about her and she'd gone with this other bloke, or seemed to be going with him. He wondered what old George would say about it, other than his usual clichés: 'Plenty more fish in the sea, mate, trouble is you gotta catch 'em.' 'You do need 'em though, dishes'll pile up without 'em.' If he was a bit pissed he'd probably say, 'It'd be like shagging an open purse if she's been married that long,' or, what he'd heard him say when they'd first met at the club, 'Like nobbin' an open French window, mate.'

It was all irrelevant though, a silly, pointless solace. Waiting for a bus, he felt increasingly embarrassed by his shouting at Gail, and increasingly regretful. He'd balls'd up, he knew it. And whoever her bloke was, he liked him even less now.

He went to Covent Garden, remembering when it had first become trendy and began with a shop selling candles, looked around a bit and, fancying a piece of cake, went to another overpriced eating place. A man, looking a bit oriental, with a WWII flying jacket and a mid-fifties quiff came in. Billy asked him if it was a vintage Irvin, he could see the three riveted air holes.

'Yeh, I only picked it up last week.'

'Like yer quiff.'

'Not as nice as yours though.'

'Well, I use Black And White and Murray's pomade don' I.'

'Mind if I join you?'

'Sit down. Where d'you get the jacket?

'Camden. You been to Greenwich Market?'

'Yeh, get some good clobber there, got a nice suit that looked the part, not a bad price either. Tell you what I got the other day, a great hand-painted acetate tie with this kind of leaf design and … ' They carried on, discussing the fashion, music, the films. He loved these impromptu meetings and conversations; they were a reinforcement; a recognition of his interests, enthusiasms, of him.

After saying goodbye to flying jacket man, he lingered a while. Jackets - and he was wearing for the first time a pale grey Minnesota woollen one that he liked himself in - hats; his two fedoras and a baker boy cap, shirts, his favourite being a dark blue Pendleton, shoes, jeans, especially his Levi's red tag, were all great. But they weren't enough.

He had friends, some he'd known for years - Christ, he and George had been in Junior school together - some women pals he saw at the club and occasionally at the monthly cake get-together one of them ran, but … even if his photography work was to do better or he could somehow buy a place that was large enough to put a museum in for his stuff: his thirties and fifties collections of Bakelite door handles and photo frames, lamps, Picture Post magazines, vinyl records - cupboards full of them - all of it, it wouldn't be enough. He left, thinking of Gail again.

CHAPTER 10

She was washing up, the warm suds-filled water offering a comforting balm as she watched the bubbles breaking and gently cleaned cereal remains from a French bowl she'd recently bought. She thought of what it would be like if he lived with her then wondered why she'd thought it. She tried to kid herself that it was a new idea. It was different with Stanley; it had seemed so natural that he came here after they'd lived together in the flat, so easy in a house she'd always known.

There were the practicalities, of course, the details, the little things involved with occupying the same space. Like now, he perhaps drying, she telling him where the tea towels were, the way she set a table if she had people for dinner - maybe he'd think a table cloth too fussy - where she kept things, in what cupboards, he would have to get used to different spaces for the saucepans, colander, the chopping board, though he didn't seem that interested in cooking, did so little of it, and perhaps he'd want the TV in a different corner of the living room, and where would he do his academic work? The smaller of the spare bedrooms would do for that, and she would have to get used to waiting for the bathroom occasionally.

It would be nice, though, to be able to touch him when she wanted - and how she wanted to touch him - even just passing in the hall, on the landing, the living room, because he would be here, not there. Thinking of touching him, she felt a warn shiver and thought of the things she had said to him and was still saying. She knew they were clichés, but as he'd told her, clichés are born of truth.

She'd told him recently that she had never felt so much for anyone before and - though still hardly believing it herself - had meant it. It had surprised her when she had said it for it had all come so quickly, the rush of feeling for him; it had been so rapid. In a rare detached moment she mused on whether she loved him or was *in* love.

Whatever it was, it was. It had covered her, enveloped her. She felt saturated with it.

There had been no one thing, no one moment or time that had caused her to feel so much, that tipped her towards him so precipitately. Sometimes it was little incidents, as when noticing the shape and length of his hand as he turned a tap, the way he casually and skilfully painted a window for her, the tidy manner in which he drank and ate, forefinger along the top of his knife, the way he closed doors softly.

Sometimes it was the bigger things; the sexual games, of course - she loved the way he expressed himself - his choices of plays, art films, a comedian or two in a room above a pub, the generosity with his time, proofing her course essays, advice on using sources outside recommended text books, listening to her moans and family tales, and he always paid for things when she was with him. It seemed both cameo and epic.

'I feel I have everything with you,' she had told him. 'You drive me mad, my feelings for you frighten me; I could kiss your body for hours.' And once, 'We've just spent thirty hours together; when you leave I'll walk around in a trance.' She could hear herself clearly saying to him that his 'just existing was sexuality itself.' Not too long ago she would perhaps have been embarrassed by saying something like that, but not now, she had experienced it, experienced him. She had received his spiritual generosity.

She had shown him a definition of love she'd found somewhere. He had written her a note criticising it, saying:

This attempts a definitive encompassing of a world, yet merely captures a few islands, like trying to hug sand or lasso water. It tries to objectify a subjective totality. It ignores the massive reality of a face-to-face confrontation wherein the *isness* of the other may take precedence over your own.

He'd signed it '10pm Tuesday evening. Vincent.'

She forced herself to return to the now. They could get some forties stuff, she didn't mind putting some of her things back in the loft, she'd be happy to live in a specific period, that one especially. They could make a room a forties space, a little world. He'd shown her some poems he'd written about the forties, you could tell he'd got it right, that he emphasised with the time, the feel of it. Maybe his grandfather or someone had fed him tales about it, or he'd read stuff that highlighted it for him. It would be fun to get the bits and pieces they wanted. He'd probably like a hand in choosing her clothes too, though he always seemed to admire those she wore when she dressed up, especially her hats.

She knew it would be a wrench for him to leave his place. The work he'd done, his garden, the concrete pool, he couldn't bring them with him, or the wall murals he'd taken so long to do; the details, the small brush he'd used with just four hairs on it. He'd told her how he'd had to chop the plaster away under the linen-backed lining paper he'd painted his butterflies on in the kitchen because he'd wanted to put them elsewhere, soaking the chunks in a bath of hot water, peeling the paper off then sticking it to squares of chipboard and virtually repainting two of the damaged ones. All that work, but at least he could bring these with him.

And there were the memories it would have for him, his ex-wife who he had never talked of except to say almost flippantly that it shouldn't have happened, that he'd been a lost child. She wondered sometimes if he still was. He had inadvertently mentioned a woman he'd had a relationship with for a while and though he hadn't expanded on that it was all more memories of the place that he would leave behind.

She wanted him to feel he had to, and to need her love above anything. She wondered if it was selfish, but she needed it returned. In the beginning he'd once left her a note on the bedside table when he'd gone early one morning when she hadn't known he was going, casually saying, 'See you Wednesday, it'll break the week up.' What it was breaking was her heart.

He hadn't rung to say when he'd get here but she knew he was coming of course. She'd boiled the kettle three times and the tea bag had been in a cup for a couple of hours. She was wearing a pair of ranch pants she'd seen in a market in Colchester - aware that British women probably didn't wear them in the forties because they were American and unavailable - and had had her hair done locally with a large victory roll in front.

She was excited, but there was a little smudge of trepidation at the back of her mind because she'd become used to having the place to herself, it was hers. She had the tiniest thought then that she might occasionally call him 'Stanley' by mistake. No, they were so different. 'The King is dead; long live the King' she supposed. This was her Queendom, one which she was happy and willing to share with her man. She looked at the larder, her usual veggie stuff: pulses, beans, tofu, cannelloni, nuts... She'd even decided to cook meat for him if he was reluctant to do so himself.

She wondered if she would need a new wardrobe - correcting herself by mentally replacing 'I' with 'we' - because she'd been acquiring more clothes, more period stuff, and was enjoying them increasingly, it pleased both of them. She often collected knick-knacks for the house, but not shopping for shopping's sake, and she wasn't one to rub her hands over material; cotton, polyester, whatever, in shops, but she was getting particular about the dresses and coats she was buying now. She had never seen Vincent dress up, he hadn't at Stanley's funeral, but of course, he hadn't known it was taking place, hadn't known her. It seemed such a long time ago.

He wasn't sure afterwards whether it had started off as a joke or not - the immediate deflection of 'Women, eh? Can't live with 'em, can't live... with 'em' came to mind - as Gail said, 'Okay then, let's go for it, come and live with me.' Adopting the persona of a playground schoolgirl, she'd added tauntingly, 'Go on then, I dare you.'

They were at his place and had been to a trattoria tucked behind Leicester Square after seeing a film. They'd been discussing what they'd seen - the chief character saying of his wife, 'She's impossible, I'm impossible, life's impossible' - when he'd started theorising on why women and men were so different.

'Are we getting to you proposing some sort of natural incompatibility?' she'd asked, and they'd continued with some rather lazy, ill-thought, though amusing ideas for a while until she'd mentioned living together.

He remembered the conversation.

'You have to decide,' she'd said, this time a little provocatively. 'Why not? I know you'll be coming to the house I was born in and perhaps you're going to say that maybe it's me that should leave, a new start perhaps, a new life, if you like, but I don't want to.'

'But I have to?'

She was teasing again. 'We can have a forties look can't we? You can hang wallpaper can't you? They also used distemper on the walls then didn't they? I'll even let you use a bit of that.'

'You'll let me?'

'Hold on.'

She went upstairs and returned holding some cardboard cylinders.

'I put these in the back of your wardrobe when I was last here; I got them from a charity shop.'

She opened one revealing a typical forties railway poster, an Art Deco feel to its stylised brightness. While he was looking at it and about to open the others, she went upstairs again and came back wearing the veiled hat she'd worn at the funeral.

'You asked me recently if I'd wear it again. I put it behind your scarves and things, I thought you might see it, it was a sort of surprise, but you didn't, did you.'

She almost sashayed to the hall mirror, turned to him with the finger tips of a hand on the underneath of the brim.

'I'll wear it any time you like. That ok?'

He knew he was being seduced, but it was a willing and almost irresistible seduction.

'I'll even let you bring your bed,' she'd said, grinning.

He'd managed a while ago to find a black and chrome headboard for his bed and also a Diomode light that reflected from the mirrors on the figured walnut dressing table he'd gotten cheap.

'Its not forties, but I want it, let's not be too purist in this case, eh?'

She smiled. 'Alright, exceptions for these two items.'

They were both quiet for a while.

'Are you thinking of the extra travelling time from the Island to your college? It'll only take forty minutes or so extra; you've had it easy with your ten minute journeys.'

He'd said nothing. They'd casually talked about the decade, she knowing more of the fashions than him, as if they'd already agreed that it was a done deal; that he would move in with her.

It had been relatively easy to say yes, here, surrounded by familiar things: his mural, tiffany lamp, the full bookshelves and built-in cupboards he'd made. He tried not to dwell on what he'd done to the place, the effort, skills, the labour of … no, not love, of a timely need, a contradictory shelter-like yet expressive escape from grinding, repetitive manual work, from living with his parents, with his ex. She had stayed with him here through the emotional and then physical separation, until she hadn't any longer; he'd also bought her out of a mortgage she'd refused to contribute to.

His gaze was wandering around the lounge and everything it contained as he thought these things. But he had tasks to do, unusually he'd let the marking pile up, there was also the relearning of chunks of theory he'd forgotten, and he wasn't going to stand in front of people offering mere outlines and telling them to refer to their textbooks for the rest.

He should also start packing; fill boxes with his possessions, with his goods and chattels, his nearests and dearests, his life so far. He should take a chance; just do it. He needed no more than her, did he? Perhaps his psyche had been metaphorically living in glass-cased formaldehyde.

He hadn't liked the first potential buyer; the quick, cursory glances at everything, Vincent knowing he was thinking of double glazing, an attic conversion, a PVC front door; a rampaging, philistine trail of aesthetic destruction. It shouldn't have mattered, the purpose being the price offered. The second had been a cockney Asian. The man hadn't taken long to make up his mind; it was all too bland for him. Perhaps he didn't have the cash to Asianify it with reds, gold, silver and embossed glass. There hadn't been any one since. It had not been on the market long.

Wanting a break from work and property, he told himself he'd do college stuff after he'd watched TV a while. Aimlessly flicking his remote, there again was someone putting food in their mouths. He'd noted before the interior and increasingly exterior scenes of dramas showing characters eating or drinking, and had perversely decided to list the number of times in a week of dramas where similar shots occurred and, while he was at it, note the amount of commercials, not necessarily for things to eat, showing close-ups of food entering mouths. If they were part educational, they failed; he knew what food was and how to eat it.

Not bothering with quantification he watched detectives standing or walking around in a police station, drinking from polystyrene cups or consuming carton'd food, talking and arguing about a child murderer they were closing in on. Were directors frightened of actors not knowing what to do with their hands or was it all in the name of realism?' If it was, why not, he thought, show close-ups of characters continually farting, pissing and shitting. The whole circus could have been part of a twenty four-seven commercial for fast food.

He'd also noticed the accents, another confirmation that far from dying, cockney pronunciation was spreading ubiquitously, especially the soft and hard 'th:' 'frew' and 'free' now dominating and a commonplace even in recorded forms at stations and airports - the 'eafrow' Express telling us that we can now 'travel free to terminal free,' and the 'v' as in 'bovver,' 'wivout,' and the glottal stoppage also the norm, including media inarticulates who say 'you know' three times in one sentence.

Perhaps, he mused, tongue-laziness was partly the cause because to put the tongue between the teeth, slightly revealing it, is tantamount to showing the inside of the body and perhaps for mythical or religious reasons, we ... He shouldn't be bothering with this.

Feeling himself growing cross again, he switched off the TV and pulled some of Gail's poems she'd written to him over the last month from the bookshelf; it eased him, a smile running into and settling inside him, the immediate antagonistic response to any lopsided cadence and grammatical errors in abeyance as he randomly selected verses from them.

There walks no dark tall man who doesn't
turn my head
there walks no stranger lean who might
be you instead
you have brought me beauty, hope in all I do
you are every colour, everything is you.

And another.

Your memory of our growing past,
your stunning intellect expressed softly,
and I feel your being in mine.
you are my God-given prize.

Knowing that if he went to bed now he would, unusually, get to sleep quickly, musing on softly written words, images of paths, sunsets, fields, the cottage through a haze of leaves, he conversely decided to go to Brick Lane for a meal; it wouldn't take long.

On the train he saw several males 'manspreading' - thinking of Gail saying that 'nobody had balls that big' - and, surprisingly tucked in a corner seat looking sheepish but serene, a young mother breastfeeding a baby, both child and mother sharing pleasure, becoming sated. He mused on whether the idea of female penis envy was an implicit conspiracy by men to hide their unconscious envy of the womb and woman's ability to create and sustain life. A cultural influence, of course, in that in a male-dominated world while it's acceptable for a woman to want what a man has, the reverse doesn't hold.

He then caught a glimpse of a Queen Anne building and thought of the one in Syon Park he'd seen recently which was soon for demolition, and ridiculously fantasised about tracing the developer, kidnapping him and treating him anthropomorphically as if he were the building; smashing his body with a wrecking ball, his head with a sledge hammer. He smiled to himself, got off the train, had a meal and returned to home and bed.

Some days later, after waking, getting to his feet and leaving the bedroom; it was easier than he'd thought it would be. The driver of the pantechnicon - though it apparently wasn't called that anymore - and his mate took his possessions out with Vincent helping and watching them load them onto the vehicle. There were quite a few boxes: books, crockery, kitchen stuff, computer, folders, miscellaneous bits of paper, and the heavier pieces: bed, desk, armchairs, table, though no sofa or sideboard; the paraphernalia of moving.

He purposely didn't look back at the house as he followed them in the car, imagining sitting on their tail board, legs swinging, and singing, 'My old man said follow the van and don't dilly-dally on the way.' He hadn't thought of that one for years.

To lighten the trip, to ease what suddenly seemed the harshness of what he was doing, he thought of other songs he remembered older relatives singing, 'You look sweet, talk about a treat, you look a dapper from yer napper to yer feet, dressed in style ... ' and, 'I do like to be beside the seaside, I do like to be beside the sea ... ' and one he recalled someone singing in a pub, 'It's a long way to Tipperary, it's a long way to go ... '

He sang the words he could remember, though not very well, a good part of the way through Essex, the rest of the journey dwelling on memories of standing outside 'The Anchor' on the corner of his street in Plaistow looking in at the yellowed silhouettes of drinkers in the public bar, with his father coming out occasionally to bribe him with crisps and hearing, amongst sentimentalising pint-raising celebrations, 'If you was the only gel in the world,' and 'It's still the same old story, a fight for love and glory' - the latter he realised now coming from 'Casablanca' and which his mother, liking old films, had taken him to see.

He hadn't understood it, but the tune came back: a soft-focus Bergman 'lah-lah-lahing' it next to Sam's piano and then the full orchestra and the timeless song. Although too young to comprehend 'glory,' he felt, standing there in chafing grey serge shorts and socks wrinkled around his ankles, a kind of gloriousness filling him. Perhaps he was partly experiencing a kind of nostalgic frisson, a sort of pre-pubescent meaning, perhaps his first sensation of some sort of childish love. But he was grown up now, leaving home to live with this woman. HIs love.

As he drew nearer he could see her standing by the garden gate. She was wearing her shoulder-padded blouse, pencil skirt and brimmed hat again; for a second he was in a dream where she was an instrument of the devil being used to ensnare him into an inescapable trap. They could turn that into a scene; perhaps he could play the devil as well. He could also picture the driver and his mate in the stopping cab in front looking at each other with an unspoken, 'Lucky bugger.'

The feeling switched as he stopped behind the van, glanced at her briefly then began taking his stuff from the tailboard and carrying it along the path to the door, she squeezing his arm in passing as she took some of the lighter bits while the removers began taking in the rest. It didn't take long; he was neither habitual collector nor hoarder.

She seemed to know exactly where she wanted everything. He hadn't thought about it, if anything he'd assumed they would decide between them where his belongings would go. Perhaps it was this that made it an awkward beginning for him, but it was one he was determined to ignore. But as he remembered a poem she had written to herself and shown him a little after last staying at his house, he was aware that the dare was a serious one for her too.

Could you leave it all for Vincent?
my place on the ground
my fortress within
all that seems sure
is also my tomb.
And holding my keys
he offers me more
my head in his lap, my heart on his palm
my life on his blade
this mourning for calm
Could I?

It seemed to be all good, really; standing at the back of a classroom watching students doing a test he'd set and thinking of what he and Gail would do that evening. They rarely watched television so maybe they'd sit on the bench in the autumn garden, his arm around her shoulders, looking at the water, setting sun, the orange-ochre leaves, thatched roof, hearing bird cries; a rustle of wind. He enjoyed the returning from work, the anticipation, the meals she cooked for him, he'd probably enjoy them whatever they were, the talk, the domestic bits - the general cleaning was hers but then it was habitual, she'd lived there a long while.

He'd decorated a room - the second bedroom, which was almost as large as the main one - in forties-style, finding some whitewash for the ceiling and papering the walls in a pale green floral pattern, though stopping short at linoleum flooring. Having more time for shopping than him, and to complete the illusion, she'd bought a few secondhand bits of forties furniture: a chest of drawers, a mahogany wardrobe too dark for his liking, an ebony wood hand mirror and other knick-knacks, and they continued their little narratives.

One he'd particularly enjoyed, on her suggestion, was a pretend class in the front room where she'd arranged a couple of rows of chairs and played a sexually aroused student watching him and listening while growing increasingly restless and excited. She'd sent an email to him at college the next day.

Deer teecher,
Fank you four the report. It woz realy unfare to give me 2 our of 7 when I've tryd so hard to pleeze you. I no I spent a lot of time looking at your shoulders, legs, eyes and bum etceterer. But that's not my falt, rite? I can't help my whoremoans.
How about meating me behind the bikesheds four extra chewition? Won day wen I'm a colidge chewtor you will be proud of me.
Gail
(one of the others, Tracey, told me your reel name is Kevin. I like you lots, Kevin, bur she dont believe you when you make me take my clothes off and say I can learn sosheology beter that way).

And a month or so ago when she'd had a family funeral to attend and stayed overnight, he'd left a brief love-letter on the mat inside the front door for when she returned in the evening telling her how desolate the house had felt, to which she'd replied:

Vincent,
Just read your note. How do you do it? I feel as if you're dismantling me piece by piece - in and out of bed - It's frightening, really terrifying. I don't like this power you have - my peace of mind, my balance, my sense of self are at issue here. This isn't just love - it's insanity.
Don't stop.

He'd be okay here; it was hers, but his, also. Maybe he could do something with the garden, though he didn't really want to, his had been a one-off; but because he hadn't constructed virtually every square inch of something didn't mean it wasn't his, did it?

He looked at his bed, he remembered buying it but it wasn't in its usual surroundings of course, they were miles away, and his butterfly paintings looked a bit ... lonely, scattered; one in this room, another in a spare bedroom and one she had put behind a large yucca in the back room, and she hadn't put any of his sketches up. He'd also noticed a rather ugly little corner in the landing that needed something done to it; and the stairs were narrow and steep, and the brass runners holding the patterned stair carpet and the barley sugar banister rails seemed an unwelcome reminder of his parents' house.

There was something about the curtains, too, they had a chequered pattern which he couldn't remember noticing in the cottage before, and the carpets, mostly fitted but a few rugs, had a purple tone which he hadn't previously been aware of, nor the too-brown and fussy lightshades.

Before, the eclecticism of the place was pleasing, romantic even; the fine details of colour, material, texture, appeared now, having spent time amongst it, less appealing. But it should have been the same, the cottage hadn't changed, except the bedroom, and he was with Gail, and she hadn't changed, had she?

CHAPTER 11

He wasn't aware of it, nor precisely - if the concept was appropriate - when it began, but ... there was something missing, absent, making him lonely, though if he'd searched himself, which, unusually, hadn't occurred to him, only later wondering why it hadn't, he probably wouldn't have come up with answers. He'd been here for months now, being loved, at times intensely so - that dulling Freudian definition of love as an 'overestimation of the sex object' inert and silent in his text book memory.

He couldn't have defined this time, it was a fog of a different sort that wrapped around the inside of him, a mist of pleasure, in which he wanted and took and was sated; they both were. He couldn't and didn't want to see into and through it, it was, or had been, a sort of craziness.

The scenarios seemed to have stopped, the last being outside of the bedroom when they'd gone separately into a pub on the Island and he'd chatted her up at the bar so convincingly that he'd noticed people around them looking uncomfortable, but had still continued it outside walking by a stream. He'd enjoyed it, but not, he felt, quite as much as he should have.

They continued the entertainments: the cinema, theatre, the occasional drink and get-togethers at college where the adolescent in him loved showing her off to colleagues, but there was something increasingly opaque blunting his senses. Then it all became slightly ritualistic, and less frequent.

After work he began, occasionally at first then almost regularly, to visit the refectory, the catering teacher getting his students to cook trout, steak, sushi, even haggis. He'd sit there thinking of her but not wanting to return to her, just yet. He realised that he looked forward more to the weekly two evening classes he was taking, and it wasn't just the stimulus of being with bright, mature students from manual working backgrounds, it was just being away from the cottage, from her.

Then her notes began. He was aware that she wasn't happy, a barely recognised sour part of him wondering if she and people generally should expect the condition to be present in their lives. She had talked of giving up her course, and also of going to see a therapist. He couldn't remember his response when she'd told him. She had. She'd stuffed a letter in his folder before he went to work one morning. He read it in the library at lunchtime.

Vincent

I am so filled with all kinds of feelings; I don't know what to do. If I try to tell you, I risk you hurting or snubbing me. When I start to speak of my emotions and you make a negative comment, you are saying that you don't like who I am; that is what I feel. I can't understand why you are against the idea of me seeing Brenda the therapist - I've only spoken to her on the phone, never met her; perhaps I won't now. You sneeringly called her 'an adventurer on a couch,' and said that 'sanity was a cosy lie.'

Do you doubt her ability; or those of therapists generally? Do you think she would make me unloving? Think that I could admire her and it would take my admiration away from you? Perhaps you feel it would be a breach of your privacy by discussing you with her or is it that you're not interested in what I experience so the quickest way to stop me talking is to criticise me? (Ugh!)

Perhaps you feel that any affection or trust I have in others means that my love for you is threatened. I've no idea if any of these are near to what you feel. My biggest dread is that you have nothing to give me, that you do not have enough energy or concern for me because you need all you have to survive psychologically.

I need to relate closely with another person for my own survival. I have stopped talking about my feelings with friends since you came. Maybe I can find a way to love you but discuss difficult feelings with a trusted confidante; there would be less intimacy and closeness but at least it is being together without my dashed expectations. If you can't tell me how you feel or listen to me, then you can't. If I tell you my feelings as they arise it's possible you can't accept me, you may leave me, or stay, disliking me. For me this is almost too much agony to even think of.

I feel at times that you've invaded me. When you let me see the landscapes of your mind, you are the most absorbing and wonderful man. Mountains, canyons - eagles and amoeba - the range of your mind has sometimes moved me to tears. But you seem to want to be a mountain and an eagle all the time; one-dimensional (this is my personal and extremely idiosyncratic view). I get fed up looking at the sky while the ground crumbles under me. I find it difficult to see you as a separate person; emotionally you have always been there throughout my life. I have just awoken to you.

When you don't listen to me I lose a part of myself. I no longer remember you as I used to know you. I don't know who you are right now. I can't live in the present on memories of the past. New ways of seeing things change what was once true of both of us. Do you know who I am today? No surprises, no shocks, no growth, no change - no life.

He looked at his watch. He should have been in the classroom five minutes ago. He'd read the rest of it later. Unsure of her last sentence, feeling tired, having, he supposed, neither the energy nor will to 'grow,' he returned to the building and his usual classroom and talked about the differing models of man presented by, amongst others, Marx and Freud.

He wanted to believe the former's view that man was born, somehow, good, but made bad by contemporary society, rather than the latter's notion of humans as naturally competitive, individualistic, self-seeking, lazy and hedonistic - the Africans of course siding with Marx immediately. He wasn't so sure of the *tabula rasa* theory of man these days; that he was infinitely malleable and educable; there was a lot to be said for Freud's paradigm.

As the room emptied he thought of his list of '101 Things I Hate' drawn up a few years previously and, seeing the cynicism having perhaps a loose relationship with Freud, having to smile as he did so.

People who chop down trees and destroy flowers so they can concrete front gardens to park their cars and save a fifty metre walk.

Celebrity - The pursuit of the talentless by the mindless.

The use of specious jargon such as, 'pro-actively managing stockholder interaction to protect mid-term,' to dramatise lives and engender spurious feelings of belonging and control and to escape the effort required in using a simpler, more precise form of language.

'At this moment in time.' (Where else could it be? In someone's knee cap?).

Social commentators who defend graffiti by calling it a 'vibrant urban discourse.'

He went to the empty refectory and continued reading the letter.

Forget the option I suggested - I don't want a safe but distant relationship; other things can occupy the space left by distance. I know what I want. I want you, but not out of reach. I want your acceptance of my moody, irrational, impatient child. I want to know who you really are. I will love you anyway whatever you choose. I would prefer an active, ongoing, living love. I suspect that you would be better with a quieter, softer love; things left unsaid to sort themselves out in time.

I don't know how to do this, am too impatient to feel good with you to leave things. I want to be heard immediately or soon after. I want to sleep at nights and smile to myself during the day. There is no right way, only our way. What's best? Find a way to let me know, I can't live my life in a hopeless emotional mess but I can adapt if I know what you need. What do you need? Can I provide it? Please be honest. Can we jigsaw our uneven edges together? Lots of questions but I'm tired and depressed with hiding.

There was some more to come. He hadn't eaten, he had an early evening class; it could wait.

It was in the same classroom but a different group. The next topic on his self-constructed syllabus was education, but he managed to voice some more hates he'd recently thought of: that the world had become one vast business-led theocracy, the fact that London spends seven times less per head of population on street cleaning than Paris, and 'Stunning Apartments.' 'Do you want to go home to be stunned?' he asked them, and education as an 'enhancement technology.' He told them of a recent university flyer he'd seen proclaiming, 'Get your 3-year degree in just 2 years and start earning money sooner.' Higher Education, he pointed out, was originally - and still should be in his particular ideological agenda - about ideas: philosophy, language, literature, the questioning of everything.

He finished her letter in an empty car park.

I love your honest flashes of revelation, your funny self-effacement, your genius at making others laugh, your strong and magnificent anger (though I haven't seen much of it!), your sense of the ridiculous, your generosity, companionship, warmth, your body, I could probably go on for pages. But you get the message. Your turn.

When he got back, late, a note saying that she was staying with Becky was in the centre of the dining table. It contained more, as if she'd found a pile of encrusted, emotional, sludge from somewhere and was pushing it at him, ramming him with it.

If you won't talk to me, feel you need to hide things then I'm not the right person for you. At this moment I'm restraining myself from packing up your stuff, putting it in a bin liner and dumping it at your real home in Chisholm Road.

He remembered her telling him once, softly, miserably, before going out to visit a neighbour, that when he didn't talk to her, felt the need to hide things, that she felt like someone whose arm or leg had been amputated. He'd gone out himself to walk the darkened lanes and try to feel her pain and while doing so had recalled occasionally lying in bed some weekend mornings and feeling the room tense as she walked grimly out, wrapping a dressing gown around her in that deliberate, beautiful way she had.

It continued:

I'm still here but you have gone, I don't know where, a thousand miles away, distant. You tell me anecdotes about merry trips and cups of tea with strange women, games of Monopoly with a lady in a garden.

He couldn't remember this, but probably he'd been just filling space he felt should be filled, after a meal, after listening to some music, perhaps about Nyla, or maybe he'd been trying, like a teenager, to make her jealous.

You stumble around with so little awareness of those around you; you drive like this, too, meandering across the road so drivers have to slow down, hoot or swerve to avoid getting hit. What are your basic myths about me? That I'm damaged and frightened and you must conceal things about yourself to protect me? It seems to me that we are locked in a struggle. It seems, in my overdramatic terms, like life or death. Anyhow, it feels very basic and important.

You keep running away from me. When you come home and don't look for me, when you leave the house and don't say where you're going or when you'll be back I feel like an abandoned child crying in the night. This is such a frightening feeling I get angry and depressed. Why do you pull away from me? Is it the risk of revelation making you run for cover?

Every line of this letter is costing me more than I feel I have. You have tried to fill my child-hungry spaces with words of love and reassurance. I'm so moved I can't put it into words. I don't know where we're going but these things are eternal treasures in my heart. Forgive me when my rawness blinds me to you. Go on and be who you need to be. We must both find our way. My love is flowing with you.

He was confused; couldn't feel her love, couldn't feel *her*, couldn't quite equate the words with her, felt too tired to. He wasn't sure whether she was staying away the whole weekend. He couldn't stay here on his own. He needed some metropolis. He put a jacket oh then went quickly upstairs to a small room - probably a third bedroom when the place was built - to see if she had sent him something, a more mundane, solid, ordinary email. He squeezed in front of his computer and saw two.

The first was from a teaching agency he'd been with for years and who he hadn't bothered to tell he wanted taken off their books and who were offering him a job on the condition that he show evidence to prove he had the ability to 'deliver sociology.' What was he supposed to do, put the subject inside an envelope and slip it under the classroom door? He'd read recently that a local authority had 'delivered' twenty thousand homes. Did they put them on huge trucks and transport them to the sites? What was wrong with 'built,' made', 'created,' 'produced?' The second was from the college, which appeared to be sacking him.

It was from a relatively new coordinator of his department. He remembered when she first came and had asked him to skew what he was teaching into self-contained little tick boxes of mechanistic obeisance and to give students more tests. He'd told her that you couldn't fatten a pig by keep weighing it and that it was a regression to primary school.

Later he'd sent her a memo pointedly saying that it was a misguided attempt to quantify the qualitative, which the establishment tended to do in order to delude itself that classification was synonymous with control. This, he wrote, 'engendered an academic and cultural ethos in which creative, intuitive intellectualism was penalised by grey people who think in straight lines and who could not comprehend any other form of mental activity.'

He thought of the science-worshipping Victorians as they industriously roamed the world classifying and naming its contents, she could have been one of them. Perhaps this was her revenge.

He read it quickly:

It was brought to my attention this week that you made a racist comment regarding a certain group of ethnic students. I have discussed this with the Principal who agrees with my opinion that your services should be terminated. You will be paid your salary for the next three months. You may, of course, return to the college to pick up your belongings.

It was signed by both the writer and the Principal.

For a second he thought it may be some kind of spoof. He looked at it again. It wasn't. Then he remembered a one-off lecture he'd given at the college for a local organisation promoting the teaching of recently-arrived African immigrants. He'd been asked, he supposed, because of his experience with students from that continent. He had, before going to the classroom, casually and with a rueful smile, said to a girl on the Admin staff that he wouldn't mention sociology to them as it was, initially, often hard work to teach Africans for they were so full of religion they found it difficult to attempt detachment.

He didn't know what to do. He got into his car and drove to Colchester, trying to take an interest in the colour of slowly falling roadside leaves, the occasional pheasant crossing the road in front of him and the cloudless sky. He caught a train to London, went to Holland Park and into a French-run Victorian bakery and coffee shop where he sat on its back terrace overlooking a churchyard and tried to decide why he liked this place and its view so much.

There was, apparently, almost one tree per head of population in London and here some of them were overhanging mansard roofs, shading a brightly lit window or showing off an Italianate tower. Even a red-brick Edwardian church, despite its stately sparseness, seemed to glow as he left the cafe and walked further along a street seeing, through the tops of trees, ridge tiles and attic windows magicked by the evening sun.

Then the realisation of what had happened slammed through semi-denial. Could the union do anything? No, it was about as useless as throwing a drowning man both ends of a rope. The

Governors? But would they not share the same morally righteous mindset of those who had the authority to get rid of him?

Trying to control his anger he sat on a front garden wall, took a folded sheet of A4 he habitually carried with him for jotting down examples he could use to highlight a theory or an essay question he might think of and began writing, scribbling, knowing that when he had finished and looked at it again in the cottage he'd probably be able to read only one word in three.

She wasn't, of course, home. He didn't like entering the place knowing she wasn't there, didn't like being there without her. He went upstairs and wrote his letter. He addressed it to the coordinator and would send it to the Principal also.

The following is a reply to your letter of dismissal. Is this knee-jerk reaction the rational behaviour of a manager? You state that I made a 'comment about Africans' to someone. And? You haven't told me what I said or what you've been told I said. You made a decision based on hearsay. Should you not have asked me what was said? I have nothing to defend and, though undeserving of the following lesson, I will explain some things to you in a way which you may understand.

Positivist sociology does not (tries not to) deal in value judgements. It attempts detachment and to treat social facts as *things.* It is a generalising enterprise. No apologies are made for this for if we do not deal in generalisations then we could not attempt a social science. The relevant social fact here is that Africans are often very religious and part of my job is to get students to question where their beliefs come from and who benefits from them.

You do not need to be a historian to know that, under the guise of an evangelical mission, Europeans exploited most of Africa. The way they did this was to spread a religion - in this case, Christianity - to gain economic and social control. Indeed, the more politically aware students know this long before they meet me, as they also know that little politics is taught in their continent below H.E. level, meaning that they often come from an anti-intellectual culture, one in which they are not encouraged to analyse nor criticise the social institutions in which they live; certainly suiting the likes of Mugabe, Kabila et al.

My comment - made in a light-hearted tone - referred to the fact that it can, at times, be a little difficult to teach Africans a social science because they are so full of religion (I've suggested this to the students themselves. They have, laughingly, agreed).

Just as the statement, 'I see a dog' is value neutral, the statement that, 'Africans are generally religious' is, likewise, value free, nowhere do I imply that the dog was either 'good' or 'bad' or that I 'liked' it or did not and neither, therefore, was the students' religiosity 'good' or 'bad' or 'right' or 'wrong.' If I was to say that Jack and Jill were, respectively, male and female, am I a sexist? That 2 plus 2 is 4 means I'm a numberist? That the sky is blue, a colourist? If I refer to you as a 'white English woman' what do I get for that, two life sentences running concurrently?

Do you have a non-arbitrary definition of racism? Perhaps we may use the catch-all definition that 'any incident is racist if it is perceived as such.' If you go along this road, of course, I could perceive you as a giraffe and ergo, you are one. Political correctness, the paramilitary wing of liberalism is, arguably, the most repressive form of ideological, social, linguistic and, increasingly, economic control since Stalin. It engenders fear, distorts reality, strangles truth and forfeits fact.

I have been lecturing on this campus for 14 years to, possibly over 50 nationalities, mostly Africans. I enjoy teaching mature students, especially the latter group - ask my Ghanaian partner - and have discussed religion frequently and the part it plays in validating both a ruling class and social inequality, including gender. ('All creatures high and lowly, God ordered their estate'). Part of my brief is to get students to question. Surely this is a prime aim of education?
Here endeth the lesson.

Perhaps he was making the intended point a little heavily but he decided not to delete his fictional relationship. He mused briefly whether the reason given for his dismissal could have been a cover for an objection to his Marxian proselytizing - an 'auto-didactic secular preacher' as a student had once jokingly labelled him. Surely not, this was 'allowed' anyway through the system officially accommodating any threat to itself, thus neutering it, in this case by it becoming part of an educational syllabus.

He left it there, there was little more to say, he was tired, he'd finish it tomorrow; though it did occur to him that he should point out that the ideology was to control not just thought but feelings - another chunk of liberal blindness: that feelings are an ontological reality, thus can't be put into an evaluative sphere. But surely this was implicit in what he'd already said.

The possibility dawned on him then that most of it wouldn't be read, the debate closed down by its readers' defensive response drawing on well-tried ammunition to label it the work of a 'phobic,' or some sort of 'ist,' conceiving of it as an obsessive 'rant.' Unable to get to sleep he got up and added a little more.

CHAPTER 12

After ringing her the following day and deciding not to leave a message, being uncertain what to say, he was restless and again went to London, almost unconsciously glancing around the station for her when he got there. He walked along Brick Lane into the East End - another early link, the club, the second time he'd seen her. He went into a pub to use the toilet, looking at a sign requesting that customers refrain from dropping anything but toilet paper down the bowl, editing and rewriting it in his head. He had just done the same with a badly scanning piece of rhyming doggerel on a Tube poster advising people not to put their feet on seats; he'd reached for his pen but hadn't bothered.

As he walked away, not sure where he wanted to go, he remembered the get-together his students had arranged for that evening to celebrate the birthday of one of them and had asked him to come. He hadn't intended to but it wasn't too far away, though before making his way there he saw a thirties cinema across the road and couldn't resist walking into the foyer. Although its original function had presumably long gone, there was enough of it left - the lamps, some walnut marquetry, curved handrails, chevrons engraved on a broken mirror - to prompt a flash of teenage excitement, anticipation.

In the pub there was a small stage to the side and on it was the girl who had organised this gathering and who was groining her mini-skirted thighs around and pushing them out at everybody standing around. The swot whose name he could never remember was next to her wearing a blonde wig and rhythmically lifting up a kilt, showing his briefs. The two Ugandans, looking like bouncers, were chuckling deeply and the Nigerian women, gold bangles and ear rings glittering, were quietly smiling.

He noticed the Ghanaian women were wearing traditional dress, which seemed to glow, as did their smooth skins, and saw the Romford Marxist leaning against the flock-papered wall frowning disapprovingly. Most of them looked very different from the way they did in class and seemed genuinely glad to see him.

He circulated, drank some wine - someone seemed to keep filling his glass - learnt more about Robert Gabriel Mugabe from an extrovert Zimbabwean student, and one of the older women came over to talk to him about what she should do after college. After a while he quickly went round to most of the others, told them he had to go and wished for them to carry on enjoying themselves.

He wasn't enjoying himself, and, after returning to the Island, felt worse when nearing the cottage, its undrawn curtains revealing a black interior, even the small porch lamp not lighting as he neared it. There'd been no calls or messages.

Feeling as tired as when he'd woken after an hour's sleep and then fitfully dozed the previous night, he woke early. Again not wanting to be in the vicinity of the cottage, he drove to Colchester, passed the 'Church of Everlasting Life,' with dark-suited African men standing outside offering their Christianising pamphlets and booming evangelising spiel while the women offered single flowers to passers-by, their children solemnly restless by their sides.

He saw advertised a railway museum 'on the edge of Constable Country' - an artist good at clouds but not people - which wasn't far away, with a Victorian building, restored steam train and carriages and a signal box; if he'd been a child he could have followed the trail of Milo the Mouse, dressed up as the Station Master and pulled the levers. When he got there he did the latter without the dressing up, yanking them heavily towards him to try to get rid of some jammed emotions.

Realising he wasn't a million miles away from the place where he'd first seen her, he drove back to the city feeling almost as depressed as he imagined he would working in a dog kennel testing flea collars.

The lights were on this time. He felt apprehensive, as if a stranger was in there, one he had to meet. She was wearing red Capri pants and a bang in the front of her hair. She'd begun laying the table, whether for two or just her he didn't know. She was nonchalant, hardly looking at him.

'Becky also likes me to dress up you know.'

'Go anywhere nice?'

'A tea dance in the town hall actually, we went to church as well.'

'God again?' His energy seemed to come back. 'The only way we can know anything - and no rationalist has yet come up with an *a priori* synthetic truth, something that tells us about the world independent of experience - is through sense data and God isn't amenable to that.'

She shook her head. 'I'm not one of your students, and you're just a ... what do you call it? Positivist. Science, science - '

'No. Science, like magic and religion, is a self-contained belief system that cannot of itself be wrong, plus what a scientific truth is today will be heresy tomorrow, their paradigms shift, 'truth' shifts.'

'Maths doesn't.'

'God created the world in seven days? Maths can only tell us something about the world when it's applied to the world, there's no numbers in nature, and everything behind the equals sign is another way of saying that which is before it. They're also analytic truths; that two chairs plus two chairs make four chairs is true regardless of whether the chairs exist or not.'

She sat down at the table; put her head in her hands.

'What sort of twisted world do you live in, Vincent?'

'Interesting, the phrase 'your world,' implying there's no such thing as reality, only realities; thus denying an absolute, yet the above statement is itself an absolute, therefore is self-stultifying in that it cannot claim privileged exemption from what it's stating.'

She stood, her chair thudding backwards.

'Stop it. Stop it,' she yelled. 'No more, no more, please.' She paused. 'You've never been at home since being here, have you. Why haven't you? You haven't sold your place have you. You've still got it.'

'I never - '

'You told me you were going to sell it, in fact, I thought you had.'

'I didn't tell you I sold it. Obviously - '

'Obviously what?'

'I suppose I was … going to see how it went with you, really, and then - '

'See how it *went*? What was I, us, going to be, a temporary arrangement? A fling? I don't understand. Tell me something I can.'

'I meant that I didn't want to burn bridges, '

''Burn bridges'? What a cliché, Vincent. 'I don't love her enough to give up my home, that extension of myself.' Is that what you mean?' You haven't brought all your stuff, the rest is still there isn't it, in the home you haven't left, are not going to leave. Are you, eh? Her voice had settled into a consistent shout.

'That's why you can't give yourself, can you, it's still there; lying there waiting for you with your books; didn't bring many with you, did you. Have you been sliding back to it, giving it the occasional kiss, a few hugs? Couldn't bear someone else sitting there looking at the murals? Ever going to cut the umbilical are you, ever going to separate from your mother?' You need a place to run to, your little nest, your little womb, that's what you've made it into haven't you, or is it the memories, were they that good? Did Niya stay with you sometimes? Did she? Any one else I should know about?'

She took deep breaths, the exhaling sounding like sighs. She quietened a little.

'You need more than me; you need your little house, your shelter. You kidded yourself that by coming here you'd thrown yourself out of your womb, been… born again. I think that's what you've tried to do. But you haven't, you're still in it, your fuckin' house. You escape, don't you, into sentimentalised images; your buildings, always buildings, sometimes I think you think more of them than you do people. They're not mysteries, you know, they're just built, you worked on enough of them, you put the mystery, the spiritual stuff on them, you lay it on them yourself, cover them with it.'

She looked away from him, turned around with her back to him then faced him again.

'You once told me you saw the film of 'Billy Liar' when you were younger, and there he was living in his fantasised world when he meets Julie Christie who actually wants to share this world with him, yet eventually he walks away from her. You told me that at the end of the film you actually stood up in the cinema shouting, 'Don't, don't.' Now you've actually found someone who not only wants to be with you but wants to share the same feelings with you, the ... fantasies, the things we talk about and do together, everything.'

Her voice rose again. 'But there's nothing more than that is there. It's not real. What of me? And if I hadn't worn those forties clothes at that fete and the demo, you probably wouldn't have wanted to know me would you; perhaps you wouldn't want to know me now if I stopped wearing them, eh? You can only love me because I'm some sort of exotic fantasy you've created, some sort of prize. But I'm not, I'm just me. Look at me. You can't can you. You're frightened of a real relationship. Are *you* real?' She narrowed her eyes, her voice quieting.

'You don't want people to feel, that's why you see them as indulgent, because you're denying being ... human. Hell is other people for you, isn't it. And your perpetual analysing. You'll intellectualise yourself away.'

She picked up the chair, turned it towards her and sat looking up at him, her chin resting between her knuckles on top of the chair, as if she was tired.

'Who are you? Your buildings, architecture, they're inside you, they nearly fill you up, don't they, you're almost made of them. Where are feelings? For other people, for me? Are you capable of love? You make fun of my qualifications, my counselling, it doesn't go deep enough, not analytical, not Freudian. And you go on about your politics, but what have you done? You talk of corporate greed, profit; you're a kind of action-less rebel hiding from any real political confrontation. You told me you went on marches at university, but it was probably the thing to do at the time, and didn't you get your men to go on a go-slow on a building site for a day once? Bet you can't remember what it was about.'

She got up from the chair and replaced it carefully, precisely. She stood there, slightly crumpled, looking at his eyes.

'I don't want you here anymore, Vincent, I want you to leave. It's a kind of inertia isn't it, for both of us; you're in abeyance, as if you're waiting, but for what? When was the last time you touched me, showed any affection? Do you remember?'

'I … This is unfair.'

'You can't, can you. What a state of affairs, to have write to someone you're living with.'

'Look, I knew you were suffering and I wanted to say something, I even wanted to write to you, but I couldn't.'

'Why? Because it would be too like some contrived, pretentious stage play and it was beneath you? Wouldn't writing something have been better than nothing? That's all you've responded with, nothing.'

Her voice was quiet but steady, a resigned sadness inhabiting it.'

'And I'm fed up with this wartime stuff. I don't like it any more, I don't want it.'

She looked at him again. 'You know where to go don't you. Of course you do.'

She quickly but calmly ran up the stairs to the bedroom. He looked towards the top of the stairs, gazing at a blank landing wall.

Sitting on the same chair she had, he recalled something she had written for him before he came to live with her.

Could you leave it all for Gail?
What must you keep,
Scared to fail?
Will you embark
On the ship of risks?

He had come aboard. It had sunk. The project he'd embarked upon, come to this. He felt paralyzed. He should have told her about the house.

It was merely convention telling him to knock on the bedroom door a few minutes afterwards; he knew there'd be no response. He did it gently for a short while without calling her name then tried the handle. He'd never noticed the door could be locked.

He knew he should attempt to talk to her, try to be honest, reassure her, at least stay there; be there when she came out of the room. He couldn't. He left the cottage quickly and drove off the Island.

It was an almost automatic response now to go to London, and there was still a part of himself that wanted to look for her as he arrived at the main line station. He needed to sit down somewhere, perhaps be surrounded by some hustle and noise. He went into the station pub and ordered a beer; he hadn't had one in a while. As he turned from the bar he saw the man who'd come into the pub he and Gail had been in months before. He also became aware that he was the man in the video clip who'd been staring at Gail in the club.

Sitting away from him at a table by the entrance he thought of her singing 'Bye Bye Blackbird,' the image being obscured by one of her in the locked bedroom, shut in by discordance, a quiet rage. What was she doing now? Sitting quietly still on the edge of the bed locked into herself? Looking out of the window? Perhaps she was in the garden, tidying, raking leaves in the dusk; using her energy to get rid of frustration, disappointment.

He felt someone near him and looked up. He wasn't surprised when he saw the cockney man, as he'd simplistically labelled him. He seemed unsteady and took a while to speak.

'I know you, don't I? Last time was in a pub in … wherever, the old market where my dad used to work.'

'Really.'

'Yeh, he did. This your regular?'

'No.'

'It ain't mine neither, just popped in.'

'Nice shirt.'

'Yeh, its an Arrow Gabanaro, bought it yesterday.'

'Takes you a long while to get ready, does it?'

'Yeh. What of it?

He leant forward closer to the table. ''eard this one? This duck goes into a pub and he's chattin' wiv the barman when this bloke comes over and says he runs a circus. He says excitedly, 'Wow, boy, could I use you,' gives the duck his card and says, 'Look, give me a ring soon, okay?' and then goes out. The duck turns to the barman and says, looking perplexed, 'What would a circus want with a plasterer?'

Vincent smiled.

'Why didn't you laugh then? Not funny? I fuckin' think it is. Don't you like jokes then? Gonna tell me why it's not funny are yer?'

'It *is* funny.'

'Why didn't yer laugh then?'

'I think you're a bit drunk.'

'So I'm a bit Brahms, what of it?'

'I'll tell you why it's funny if you want.'

'Gonna explain it are yer?'

'Yes. Jokes are always about rule-breaking, being unaware of social norms. The duck sees it as perfectly okay that it - and perhaps other ducks - can talk. What surprises it is not that the circus owner thinks it would be a money-earning sensation to employ a talking duck - he misses that completely. What he can't understand is why, as a plasterer, he could be of use to a circus. It signifies an unawareness of the norm that ducks don't talk; it's the perception of the extraordinary as the normal that's funny.'

'Fuck me, d'you have to get everything right, I bet you use cue cards at house parties.'

He bent over the table and put his face closer to Vincent's.

''ere, I heard that Gail was living with someone. Wouldn't be you by any chance, would it?'

'She sends her regards.'

'What d'yer mean? I don't understand. You patronisin' me? You takin' the piss?'

He seemed suddenly to lose his footing and fell noisily across the table then to the floor. The noise echoed, drinks sloshed, glasses bounced on the carpet. Vincent stood to go around the table to help him but someone from the bar came across and got him to his feet. Vincent could see he was okay, though briefly catching his eyes saw that they were almost vacant.

He thanked the helper and left the place; there was no point in staying. He felt only a little perturbed, more annoying was that it had been something else added to his increasingly burdensome present.

CHAPTER 13

Again, he wasn't sure where he was going, though somehow it didn't matter much. But he felt he should go home; aware as he thought it that he didn't mean the Island. It didn't take him long. He had the keys with him as always. He wondered if she'd ever noticed they were in his pocket. It smelt musty, but it was nice to see the wide hall and feel the length of the through-lounge, also the green and white neatness of the kitchen and, from its window, the conifer at the side of the pool, the damson tree beyond. The bedroom seemed empty, no white-painted chest of drawers, no bed, a darkish patch under where it had been which he'd get cleaned some time, and the slight lines on the wall marking where some of his sketches and a painting or two had been.

He switched on the radio he'd purposely left there; more hyperbole: someone who had a bit part in a soap referred to as a 'star' and a Premier League footballer who, after ten games for his club, was now a 'legend' and after another ten would probably write a 'my autobiography.' He was back in his enclosed psychic valley, his trough of iconoclasm. He went out, locked the door and began his way back to the cottage, feeling lost, moving between two alienations, between Scylla and Charybdis.

Waiting for a train he consciously delayed thinking about some of the things Gail had said to him, then when it arrived, stepped into a carriage and immediately noticed a large woman, her eyes glazed with pleasure, eating a foul-smelling pile of minced food from a polystyrene carton.

Smacking her lips loudly, she dug into her bag for the finger-prodding, stroking pleasure of a phone, hardly cognisant of people around her or perhaps even that she was in a carriage, conscious only of the movement of the food repeatedly entering her gullet and stomach and the taste filling her throat. I am woman, sate me. He thought of Gail talking about feelings, *her* feelings; feel, feel, feel.

He watched the woman with an almost repellent fascination; the process of devouring, the hedonistic, indulgent pleasure, the insular unawareness. He had tentatively sat. He stood, walked towards her and stopped by her side.

'That is disgusting,' he said, pointing to the food. 'This is public transport. *Public,*' he repeated.

She looked up, startled. 'Go away.' She waved her hand dismissively. 'Go away. You are being racist.'

He hadn't noticed her colour, he could see now that she wasn't white.

'Are you going to play the race card then?' he asked in mock innocence. 'I'm not a racist, I'm a smellist.' knowing as he said it how ridiculous his self-labelling rhetoric must have sounded.

'Go away,' she said again. 'Go away.'

A man on a seat opposite her raised his face to him and said, 'Don't you think that's a bit offensive?'

Vincent turned to him. 'And I'm offended at you being offended, which you're not anyway, you're just enjoying feelings of self-righteousness and patronage on behalf of those you imagine, in your perverted little mind, may be. You're so primed to be offended you get confused about what it actually is you're offended about.'

He looked down at the woman again. 'It's essentially about the two freedoms, you see,' he said patiently, 'freedom to and freedom from: you want freedom to eat your hot, stinking food on public transport, I want freedom from suffering it.'

He was standing near the carriage through-door. He grabbed the handle, yanked it towards him, pushed the next door open and marched through to the adjoining carriage. Hearing someone shouting into his phone, he went into the next one, slamming its door behind him. As he did so, he could smell the sharp, nauseous tang of vinegar.

Halfway along the carriage was a man of about thirty wearing a cement-splattered shell suit, his feet on the opposite seat and dipping chips from a paper cone into a splodge of fried sugar and ascetic acid and throwing them into his mouth as if shovelling evil into it, its slurping, sucking substance seeming to enter all of Vincent's senses.

'Hey, that's disgusting,' he shouted as he marched towards him. The man looked up, bemused.

'What is?

'That is,' Vincent said, shouting still and pointing to the food. *That* is.'

'I know my rights, mate,' the man said with cheerful certainty, 'there's no law saying I can't eat on public transport.'

'Oh dear, am I infringing upon your human rights then?' Vincent asked in a wide-eyed parody of pity. 'That *is* a shame. Any idea what they mean? Don't you think they're rather arbitrary and selective?'

He took a breath and said, in a quieter, more measured tone, 'If someone kicked me and I then punched them and the action was objected to, surely I can say it was justified and therefore to attempt to prevent my action or punish me for it would be infringing upon *my* human rights, wouldn't it? In fact - '

Vincent took two strides towards him, grabbed the package of chips and pushed them into the man's face; pressing and turning them, smearing them over his features, his forehead, his hair, and while dong so a little lighthouse of detached observation was illuminating the question of whose face it actually was. His father's? He wasn't going to intellectualise this. The constant, relentless awareness of his actions, his thoughts, wondering why and where they came from and analysing them in discrete lumps of introspection, he pushed aside.

This was real, physical, the man's face covered with squashed, yellow potato as his attacker's open hand pushed into it, its circular movements flattening the nose. Vincent drew his arm back and punched it, quickly, sharply, hard, and saw the streak of blood instantly mingle with the soft vegetable. He wanted to keep punching, but stopped himself. He walked quickly away, turned his head briefly and saw the man spread his hands over his face to wipe the mess off. He then looked at his attacker angrily, stood up, took a step towards him then stopped, hands clenching at his sides, mangled chips and globules of red sauce scattered around him. He moved forward again till a passenger, seemingly for the man's own good, stood firmly in front of him.

The train was slowing for its next stop. Vincent moved quickly through to the carriage in front then the one in front of that, people jerking their heads up as he entered them as if he were an authority figure; a ticket inspector, a transport copper. He was first out of the door as the train halted and moved quickly along a platform, almost running up stairs then into a ticket hall and out of an exit.

He needed food, coffee, his blood sugar was low. There was a greasy-spoon nearby. He wasn't going there; more ketchup, brown sauce; open mouths chewing, talking; spluttering. A bus stopped, he got on knowing an innocent baguette-and-brie place awaited at the end of its journey. The sun, breaking through clouds, illuminated the cannon-lip chimney pots of large-gardened roadside houses, on the other side was mostly parkland until terraced streets with tall pavement trees ran straight and long at right angles from the main road.

He felt a little calmer by the time he walked into the café and sat, noticing as he did a trace of blood on the back of his hand. He shouldn't have done it, but didn't *feel* as if he shouldn't have done it. Perhaps, he smiled to himself, he hadn't; nobody had come after him from the train, though he had got off it quite near the steps and had jumped on a bus almost immediately he'd arrived outside the station.

A waitress came and when his request was answered by the ubiquitous 'No problem.' he felt an instant annoyance.

'Should there be?' he asked. 'It's a café, it's owned by a Frenchman, you've got coffee beans from five continents; you have cream, milk, sugar, the loudest *Gaggia* machine in the world. *Should* there be a problem?'

He looked down at the floor, took a breath, watched her start busying herself with his order and was about to apologise then decided not to bother.

Though not enjoying the food, he felt a little better as he went out and walked along next to the freshly painted Mediterranean azure of a Cycle Super Highway - a euphemism for the sponsored aesthetic vandalism of the city's roads - and turned down a side street to get away from it, feeling a tenseness as his body responded to a short, loud, rhythmic hooting from a car whose driver had stopped outside of a house. The klaxon-like sounds were repeated, reminding him of being woken several times over the years at six a.m. by a similar sleep-startling noise. He marched over to the vehicle and thumped on the side window. The driver looked surprised and wound it down.

'Why can't you get up and walk ten yards to the door and ring the bell instead of disturbing half the fucking street? Does the concept of other people have any meaning for you?' He heard himself getting louder. 'Eh? Does it?' He pushed his hand in and grabbed the man's shirt collar. 'Does it? he shouted, pulling the neck and face towards him.

He released the collar, gripped the man's hair and slammed the face onto the bottom rim of the opened window. He lifted the head and repeated his action, seeing, as he pulled the head up, a neat red line joining the eyebrows and which started to smudge as blood began oozing from it. He let go of the hair, went back to where he'd been walking and continued along the road, his pace quickening. He looked briefly back; he could see the driver's head moving about; he'd be okay.

Looking towards the end of the road in front of him he saw a glint of water, there was a canal there; he'd walk along that. He began running towards it, slowed down as he went through a thick coating of leaves and onto the towpath, not sure whether he felt exhilarated or awful. What had he done to that man? And the one before him? But they had it coming to them, didn't they?

He walked steadily along the path noting an unprepossessing, uncared-for house with shallow pediments above pseudo-Georgian windows and again wondered why Victorian architects, with the embellishments of colonial masturbation, had enjoyed destroying the perfect proportions of a twelve-paned box sash.

He watched a father and son cray-fishing under a grafitti'd bridge and, unusually for canal-side homes, walked past privet hedges, scrolled gates and the black and white diamond tiles of front paths. Two of the houses had fan palms and monkey puzzle trees with the rich green leaves of others almost hiding *fin de siècle* gables.

He imagined people of the period: goggled motorists, a plaid lapel entrepreneur, maybe a waist-coated Chief Clerk smiling up through branches in the bright jade light, though on the other side of the waterway, east, trees would be knuckled, dry, council-pollarded. He pictured a coalman bending sacks on his shoulder over a doorstep chute; below, a boy standing on the settling coal, cellar blurred by dust then running out to a horse pulling a carted carousel with rides for jam jars and shrimps and winkles from a nearby barrow.

His mother, the apple of a street bookie's eye, a daily herring and bowl of tea seamstress sewing leg of mutton sleeves and lining merry widow hats, watches her son playing in a sandpit and, looking up, glimpses in the distance a veranda, mullioned windows reflecting the sun, high chimneys, a sunlit, jacketed shoulder on a camomile lawn, and the splendid trees...

He carried on; willows, gravel, the sun, then the impatient crunch of cyclists behind. They weren't ringing their bells and had probably adopted the view that as they now 'share' pavements' they could also do the same thing with canal tow paths. He stuck to the centre for a while then stepped stubbornly to the left. After hearing a a slide of braked tyres, he wandered to the right as a bandana'd girl moved past, her handlebars hitting his elbow, then a fat, tattooed man ground into his side, shoulders hunched in annoyance.

Vincent strode two steps forward to grab his t-shirt and try to lift him up - though instantly aware he wasn't strong enough - imagining the man treading pedals no longer there as his bike slowly fell, but there was no need; he veered suddenly to one side and dropped on his back, heavy and surprised. The girl turned her head, quickly laid down her cycle and ran towards her partner. She knelt beside him and began dabbing his grazes with a handkerchief, looking up and frowning at Vincent as he passed by them and continued on.

Things seemed to be going well, he didn't even have to touch this offender; he had got his comeuppance by accident. He walked further, passing a small playground and the squeak of a swing as a laughing child left it for the next excitement, then, coming towards him, looking eagerly at him, were a group of Africans who he guessed were Jehova's Witnesses - as they came nearer he could see the stationery they were waving about were copies of 'The Watchtower.'

Every time they'd descended on his street like a plague of locusts and knocked on his door with hotlines to god and a proselytizing routine that, with another I.Q. point, could have been a plant, he'd promised himself that in the face of another ecclesiastical onslaught he would smile patiently and either shut the door or run away. This time their fellow believers greeted him warmly and asked if they could speak to him for a moment. They were courteous; smiling warmly as they gently surrounded him. He asked them what they were doing on a canal.

'We wanted to enjoy the sun and the water,' was the reply.

He told them pleasantly that he wasn't a believer, that it was pointless to try to convert him, that he envied their belief and hoped they would continue to enjoy themselves. As he walked on a man came from the direction of the playground and began speaking to the group. Vincent could hear him distinctly say, 'Any trouble here at all?' Nothing negative was said to you was it?'

Vincent couldn't understand what he meant. He walked back and asked him. The man was tall, wearing a linen shirt and jacket.

'I just wondered if you may have been objecting to whatever they were doing, that's all. They do, of course, have a right to do whatever it was, maybe it was religious or something, I don't know, but nevertheless we do need to assimilate other cultures do we not?'

Vincent asked him what he thought he had said to them.

'Oh, I just wondered, that's all, we must respect differences musn't we? Their mores, customs, etcetera?'

The man suddenly became the quintessence of a hubris-ridden attempt to elevate further the current moral universe, the current hegemony. Vincent moved nearer him.

'Oh, I see,' he said with exaggerated politeness. 'We are asked to assimilate all cultures are we, writing the idea of 'when in Rome' out of history of course. That's very accommodating of you I'm sure.' He smiled then suddenly pointed along the canal behind the man.

'Oh look,' he yelled, eyes wide in mock horror. 'There's an adulterous Somalian woman being stoned to death on the pavement. Yeh, let's give it up for Sharia law!' He gleefully punched the air.

The man turned towards the direction of the pointing finger. He looked startled.

'Your liberal heart can't face reality can it,' Vincent shouted, 'it's too comfortable pumping away in dreamland. Stop trying to control people's feelings, your attempt at some sort of psychic totalitarianism. You are dangerous. Go. Now.'

Vincent turned and went on along the path, hearing the satisfying sound of trodden stones beneath him. He walked for a while, he was on his own now, no cycles, people, proselytizers, except himself, but the incidences were unsettling him, all of them, and he didn't want to dwell on them. He needed escape, to immerse himself in something, to inhabit it.

He went up the steps of another canal bridge and walked along a narrow but busy road to its junction with a wider one and saw a small cinema. The film, which had only just started, he hadn't seen for years. Perhaps people had noticed what he'd been doing and would be looking for him; maybe he should go into it anyway and pretend he was a fugitive escaping the law, the idea had an appeal.

After the movie had ended he sat motionless, wanting to hear the theme music again and perhaps even to see who the second assistant director was before the shock of an empty black screen and reluctantly having to accept the need to leave this warm, dark space and face the harsh light and the traffic outside. Then someone sat directly in front of him, heavily, he could feel the seats around the man shake. He was obviously here for the next showing. He had a large funnel of popcorn and began eating hungrily, the munching noise getting louder. Vincent bent forward, the side of his face almost touching the man's ear. He began quietly.

'I know the film's ended but I'd like to listen to the music and concentrate on the credits. Is that okay?'

He was ignored. A little louder he said, 'Look, you can't just do what you do at home in a cinema, you're not in your front room.' Again there was no response.

'If you don't stop eating for just another couple of minutes,' said Vincent casually, 'I'll throw your supper all over the seats or perhaps jam them into your face.'

The man turned around, frowning. 'You'll bloody what?'

Vincent leant over the seat, grabbed the container and shook its contents over the man's head, some of the popcorn staying there, the rest settling on his shoulders and lap. Without waiting for his victim's reaction, aggressive or otherwise, he moved along the row of seats into the aisle and towards the exit. The small audience had gone, only a woman in casual uniform wearing headphones and picking up empty drink cans from under seats was present; she had, probably, seen and heard nothing.

He looked back; the man was alternately brushing the remains of his meal off himself and looking back up the aisle. He then went into and up it towards his assailant who stood there facing him. He stopped a few yards short of Vincent then barged past, almost knocking him over, and saying in a low, tense voice, 'Prick.' and pushed into the foyer.

Vincent had always thought that if he got physical or resorted to swearing in situations like this then he'd lost the argument anyway. No, he hadn't lost this one, or the others. As he himself went through the foyer, not seeing the man, he wondered why he didn't feel upset about the happenings of the last two hours, he knew he should have been, instead he felt... freer, almost satisfied.

He decided not to go to the cottage, He rang Gail, there was no answer and he was loath to leave a message. He sent a text asking if she was okay, which seemed weak and pointless even as he sent it.

Back in the house he went to the bedroom, forgetting for a second there was no bed, but there were some old blankets in the attic and a pillow and rolled-up duvet in the airing cupboard and he got to sleep quickly and easily enough in the spare room - not wanting to use the main bedroom till his bed was back there.

In the small hours he woke with strong, detailed images of what had happened, what he had done during the day. He went to sleep again, feeling apprehensive now, wary, cautious; and guilty.

It was his job, or lack of it, he thought of as soon as he was awake, looking at the ceiling he'd painted like a starry night sky with the top of the Chrysler building in a corner pointing to its centre for guests to appreciate; there had been few. The students.

How would Victoria Agyeman and Patience get on without him? They needed encouragement, time spent on them, who was there to teach his subject? He'd miss his colleagues, the refectory, the staff room; this was usually a chattering chorus of pedagogy, a communion of roles across coffee spilt tables.

He thought of Pete lording it over his empire of three desks, grin legitimating his loveable crassness, Durham accent ruling okay as he gleefully repeated how lucky we were that evolution had got it right by giving us thumbnails so we could scratch our arses, and Alan, head of the department, provincial man, established victim, cold wife, colder kids, a Co-op ceilidh the highlight of his month. It was ordinary, familiar, almost incestuously so. And there was the librarian, who was possibly one of the few members of staff who had read Vincent's parody of Edu-biz buzzwords and phrases in the house magazine, '... proactive encouragement of student-centred assimilation of conceptual bridges to facilitate non-arbitrary criteria of recourse-based parameters for... etc.' and realised it was a parody.

If it happened, it was more familiarity gone, more security. Perhaps he *had* attempted to throw himself out of the womb and maybe, just maybe at the very time when he needed to run back to it, the solid, warm haven he had created, he should truly leave it, erupt from it; explode from it. He could move away, miles away, another country perhaps. He'd been to a few; it would have to be a city though.

He got up, made some breakfast and thought of some of the places he had been. Rome and the sting of sun at Ciampino where the cab drivers shouted and pushed each other as they waited for fares that never seemed to come, and in the city an old aeroplane droning around with a *'Vota Forza Da Liberta'* banner fishtailing above the *Teatro Dell 'Opera* where the bourgeoisie clapped themselves for being there, and the touting accordionist hissing at his saxophone rival outside the Nouvea feast of O'Brien's bar. And Paris, its street grills gushing water along culverts washing cobbles all day, its boulevard trees almost touching eaves and scrolled verandas, but not quite close nor tall enough to see from the Sacre-Coeur.

At the insistence of a friend, he'd been to Krakow and seen the prostitutes at the back of Glovny station, with their red gash of mouths, black-lined eyes, tops of breasts like white eggs, and their fee chalked on the soles of their shoes and raising a foot to catch trade from passers-by, commerce scratched away on a pavement should the police come clumsily grabbing. He remembered the Barcelona street where the statues weren't real, they were people standing still, till the chink of coin elicited an arrogant turn of head from a marble-veined Columbus or a smirking salute from a copper cast G.I. and there was a bronzed centurion who raised his spear and a golden pair of potentates who bowed as grinning tourists dropped their cents.

And Madrid; its Art Nouveau and god. His European languages were non-existent but he'd always enjoyed the trilling 'r' and elongated vowels of Italian; he was capable of learning the language.

He began mentally rounding up some of his American experiences with a kind of pointless nostalgia, knowing he could never live there. The subway to Brooklyn and 'Speedy's Deli' for brunch - eggs over, rye, easy on the cheese - a neon-splattered night from the top of the Empire State, the Chrysler glistening in a humid eighty degrees, Grand Central and sunbeams, imagining Brando toughing it on Pier 17, sailors in threes on the town in Times Square and almost hearing the New Jersey accent of a Cagney cop.

There was Downtown Seattle and the market under the rooftop Cantina with its samba band and hip-swaying Mexicans - the creaking arses of the English tourists just missing the beat - and Bainbridge Island harbour and its techno-rich, high-bridged yachts with names like 'Ratpack,' 'Poodie Gal' and 'As Time Goes By.'

No. They were too far, too distant from bucolic parks, stuccoed Chelsea-Kensington, magnolia gardens and magic mews, from the glitter of a canal, steepled skylines, chimneys, Sunday best Africans marching to church, a low sun flooding the Thames, and fingers and thumbs framing a Georgian window; a thousand pictures never taken.

CHAPTER 14

As he neared the cottage he saw it was dark again. Was she staying with her friend still? At least his bags weren't piled outside; she obviously hadn't succumbed to an urge to dump them there. He inserted his key and turned it. The door wouldn't fully open. He pushed it and stepped into the hall. There were cardboard boxes piled in a row as if pushing aggressively towards him. He couldn't understand why they were there until he recognised them as his own, looking just as full and heavy as when they'd arrived. She'd obviously taken the chance that he wouldn't be here when she'd packed them. He looked into the front room. There were more, stacked up ziggurat-shaped, like the stepped-back top of a thirties building, perhaps she'd purposely arranged them that way.

A part of him wanted to stay there and sit on the top box, swing his legs like a little boy and cry 'Mummy, mummy' when she came back into the house and hold his arms out for her to pick him up, just to disorientate her. He looked at it again and pictured himself sitting aimlessly swinging his heels then digging them into it and kicking back faster and faster, stopping himself in case it became a whirlwind of kicking and hammering his fists into the packed cardboard.

He'd have to organise a van, he'd do it in the morning. What did she think he would do with his bed, chop it into pieces and put them in his boot? It seemed pretty obvious that she wasn't returning for a couple of days, but what if he was here when she got back?

He had the thought that she would be secretly glad to see him here; that it meant he now wanted to talk to her; was prepared to discuss what sort of relationship they wanted and whether it was achievable. But it felt too… logical, almost calculated, an arrangement. He wasn't any good at this. He looked about him, could see the lights of buoys and small boats through the window. He'd miss this view, as he would others, but he'd tried to make the place his home, of sorts, for months. It hadn't worked. He had to admit he now felt a little frightened of her, the image of her; woman as Madonna or wicked witch, she was now the latter. Their little stories, the, at times, almost debilitating bouts of laughter they'd shared, the way she looked in her dresses and hairstyles, the role-playing and period constructs, her appreciation of things he'd said, had done, of just being him, had now ended.

He arranged for a large van to pick him and his possessions up the next afternoon and decided to keep where he was overnight. He didn't know whether he would stay with her again, he certainly wouldn't stay on his own. He lay on his bed - it wasn't theirs, it was his - thinking of more things she'd said to him.

'There was,' she'd said the day after they had stood at the end of the garden watching the setting sun at Solstice, 'a moment yesterday that was so perfect I would happily have died, because nothing could ever be as good.' and 'I want to keep your body just for me; lock it up.' and lying with her head in the hollow of his shoulder saying that she wanted to move her furniture in there, 'my shoulderhouse.'

He'd written a poem for her, he could remember some of it.

You wanted to move your furniture in you said,
all your goods and chattels
into the slope of my shoulder, which perfectly fitted your head
and where I ran through your hair with bitten nails.
you wanted to live there permanently
your forehead on my cheek.

He recalled a few more lines before dropping into a spasmodic sleep.

You completed a jigsaw puzzle of my profile,
bathed nightly in my clavicle's hollow
and brushed your hair with the curls on my chest.
But you no longer live in my shoulder,
you have moved out, stripped it bare
and now dwell in your own being
where I follow you around looking for myself.

Billy was aware he'd managed to get home safely due to the generosity of the bloke who'd picked him up from the pub floor. The cabdriver had helped him to his door and he'd reached his bed through a haze of stop-go attempts at stair climbing. He didn't even think of his camera till he made an unsuccessful try to pull the eiderdown over him and could feel part of it about to be squashed under a buttock.

He woke as the sun rose hovering outside his curtains and, feeling as if a wall was being constructed in his head, breakfasted from his range of cereals. 'I'm a serial killer, I could murder a bowl of porridge,' he mumbled to himself as he ate. He looked down at his shiny black shoes and the beer stain on a turn-up of his jeans and one on a knee.

He couldn't remember much of the evening, he'd just fancied a drink after visiting the mother of a recently departed friend and, finding he could retrieve a year's worth of voicemail messages her daughter had left him, had put them on a disc and presented it to her so she could hear her offspring's voice whenever she chose.

He wasn't sure why he'd drunk so much, but it was a little unusual to be in a pub on his own and he had, he admitted, been thinking of Gail. He fancied her more now after hearing that she was living with someone who he still thought was the bloke in the pub the other month. Then he remembered it was the same bloke he'd talked to the night before, though couldn't recall what they'd said except him going on about a duck. He was a talker he reckoned, could probably send a glass eye to sleep. He hoped he'd said something nasty to him, he didn't like him, and where'd he got to? He'd just left him on the floor, that sort just looked down at you and did nothing.

He knew her address. He'd asked Rihad for it under the pretence that he was going to transport a couple of her big paintings, apparently she worked on them in a shed at the bottom of her garden, and had mislaid it. He'd been thinking about her a lot lately. He could have gone on about the things that attracted her to him: the smile, talent, her body, and she did look something in the forties clothes he'd seen her in, though she'd have looked even better in fifties stuff like a Jolie Moi retro or T Bird Cutie. But it was more than that, and more than the fact that he was pretty lonely, despite people telling him how gregarious and 'sociable' he was.

What if he went to see her? Not actually knock on the door perhaps but just be around where she lived, and sort of accidently bump into her. He could say that he was visiting the Island for a weekend break, that somebody had told him all about it: the water, the boats, the pubs, all sorts of things he could say to her when she asked him why he was near her cottage.

It couldn't be too obvious of course, he'd tell her that he knew she lived on the Island - she'd told him that way back - but not what side of it or exactly where it was. He could always say that he'd gone there 'cos he'd heard a lot about the local ale, the oysters and mussels, and that his granddad used to swear by the place; no Clacton, Margate or Southend for him, it was 'The Island.'

He'd go tomorrow. He could spend an hour or so before he went with his old Regentone and, as always, pleasingly anticipating the short silence and the hiss of the needle before the sound, maybe put on a few Ricky Nelson and Wanda Jackson records. He'd get a train to Colchester then a taxi, he'd treat himself.

The cabbie seemed a nice bloke; he was Syrian and had been living here a few years now and told him about his wife, parents, kids and, recognising Billy's accent, asked him to tell him some slang terms.

'Alright. Well, I met this geez the uvver day, I think he was bit light on his feet meself, a real News of The World he was, and I told him to shut his gate 'cos 'e were a bit pony and... Before you translate that, Mohammed, in the not too distant future I'm gonna have to ask you to stop so I can take me old spam javelin out and siphon me python.

'I know what the last bit means,' said the driver, and in a passable imitation of an East End accent said, "'avin' a giraffe aintcha?'

They both laughed till Billy had the idea that they weren't going the right way, somehow he felt they shouldn't be in this country lane, having no idea why. He communicated this to his driver.

'I think you are right,' he said, 'Sorry.' and did a sharp turn. Billy knew little of driving but felt immediately apprehensive as he saw a large white van directly in front swerve away from them. He could see at once that its attempt wouldn't be successful.

She'd had to do it; she really couldn't have gone on the way it was. She'd thought about it, in pain, anguished about telling him. She and Becky were about to go to a restaurant when her friend asked her what was wrong. She'd told her as best she could, though it hadn't been planned. There were no tears, there was no point. She'd halted any crying after telling him to leave. Becky had told her that if any help was required she need only ask.

'I'm going to ring him at the cottage.'

Becky had gone into the kitchen while she did so. She'd made them coffee and returned to the room with it.

'There's no answer, I can't remember him being on his own there before, perhaps he's staying away and it's obvious where. Perhaps he won't l eave. I don't know.'

She'd considered a while. She'd thought of when she had first asked him to live with her, she hadn't rehearsed it, hadn't thought about it much, and then, capturing that same feeling of decision, turned to her friend and said, 'Remember me saying what I'd like to do with his stuff? I think I should do it now, he won't be there; it would be done, clean. Want to help?'

Gail had driven them back to her home where, under her instructions, they immediately and systematically began putting his belongings in the boxes from the loft they'd originally come in. She worked quickly, glad someone was with her, not just for the carrying and packing, but to stop her looking more closely at the objects they were handling; what memories this particular one held or what that one meant, realising whilst doing so that she hadn't painted a thing since he'd lived with her. While busying herself she mused on whether she would, or could, actually go through with it if she was on her own. She gave only a cursory glance at the bed.

She was tired when they'd finished, yet knew she wouldn't stay the night, he might return and she couldn't subject Becky to any scene that might occur, and to stay here picturing the piled boxes downstairs - a mute testimony to a helter-skelter journey that had tripped and slowed, rolling jerkily downwards into a tundra - would have left her feeling like a contortionist dying in his own arms.

This was her home, yet she felt perversely as if she was the one being thrown out. She would come back to it and this would never happen again. She would think of Vincent often, but there were always the memories of Stanley, always.

Vincent had just tentatively stepped down from the van where he'd been sitting next to its driver and was now looking at a car six metres away with a smashed, steaming front end, the cause of which had filled the cab with a jagged, shattering, metallic scream and his seat belt to seemingly bisect his chest and wrap around his spine. The driver's door was open at an angle, hanging; swinging slightly from one hinge, and lying under it on the road was the driver, a darkish-skinned man moving his head a little from side to side, his face rubbing on the asphalt.

The van driver was already out of his vehicle and kneeling by the man, who pointed past his battered car and in a voice Vincent could only just hear, said, 'Him. Him.' and tried to move his arm. The van driver moved quickly around to the far side of the vehicle, the door of which was concaved. Huddled diagonally over the steering wheel was a passenger with blood dribbling slowly from his mouth.

Bending over the man lying on the road, Vincent asked lamely whether he could do anything for him. The man turned his head slowly then back again, once more scraping his face on the road. He went around the other side of the car where his driver was on a mobile describing to somebody where he was and what had happened. He asked Vincent if he was alright and to get a bottle of water from the glove compartment of the van. He did so, giving it to the van man who took a few swigs and said, 'The guy in there's in a bad way. Hope they're here soon.'

Vincent felt useless. He looked in the van again, took the keys out for something to do and gave them to their owner. Then there was the wailing screech of an ambulance and the beginning, further way, of the sound of a police car.

After being looked at briefly by the paramedics, the figure inside the car was gently pulled out, eased onto a stretcher and carried into the back of the ambulance. There was blood around its mouth. Vincent didn't recognise Billy immediately. One of his eyes was open. He hadn't noticed the colour of them before, though he recalled his shirt, an Arrow Gabanaro, its wearer telling him its name the last time he'd seen him, he wasn't sure why he'd remembered it. On that occasion his lips had been wet with alcohol; now it was blood.

He was aware of coincidental occurrences, other than the trivial ones that occasionally happened when he was thinking of words such as 'recusant' or 'manoeuvrability' and then a second afterwards hearing them from the radio, and of course the more unusual ones where the odds were greater.

He'd read of a man seeking his sister who had been adopted forty years previously at three months old who had found her after a long investigation. She noticed when he took her to his home a recent photograph of him and some friends in a park with her walking past in the background. And of twins separated at birth who had first and second wives with the same name and had male children they gave the same first and second names to, and both had dogs called Troy. He was cognisant of these happenings, but this one had just happened to him.

As he watched the ambulance disappear along the road with the car's driver also inside, its wailing seeming even louder, a police car braked sharply to a stop a few yards from the wrecked vehicle. As two officers got out, the van driver nodded in the direction of he vanished ambulance.

'I'm feeling a bit lucky, more than those two could say. I think one of 'em's okay, but the other... ' He turned to Vincent. 'Don't suppose you heard what the feller who got him out said, did you. He said it to his mate sort of casually. 'This one's dead,' he said.'' He shook his head.

One of the two constables, glancing at the van, asked who the driver was. Vincent walked away from them as they conversed; knowing that he, also, would be asked what had happened but would be able to tell them very little, he'd been looking out of the side window when they'd crashed. He thought of his belongings, but assumed they were safe; he and the driver had made a solid job of stowing, with belts anchoring some of them to the floor. The van didn't seem to be much damaged except for its dented front, and he hoped after the police had left that they could continue their journey.

He thought of the dead man and felt guilty. He knew he could be made to feel guilt - that most corrosive of emotions - rather easily, but nobody was forcing him to feel it now. He hadn't, though, been particularly nice to the man who was, apparently, dead and now nearing a hospital somewhere, soon perhaps to be taken into its mortuary. There was no logical reason why he should have been friendly towards him on the two occasions they'd met.

The rest of the journey was slow and steady, the van's occupants saying little, the driver mentioning the police and whether they believed him about the part he'd played in the accident. Vincent told him what he'd told the officers, how unfortunate it had all been, not mentioning that he knew the deceased - thinking what an impartial, dulling word that was.

He asked himself if there had been children, a wife, a mother involved in the main's life, guessing somehow that there wasn't, but there would be friends, people like him; but what was he really like? The question seemed almost a non sequitur, how do you define someone? Vincent didn't feel he cared about an answer.

The lifting and carrying of boxes and domestic objects felt an anti-climatic, mournful affair, their carriers moving around still in a state of shock to varying degrees, especially the driver. When

171

they'd finished and Vincent fed him and offered him a bed for a while instead of immediately returning to his office or home, the offer was refused though the man thanked him generously. Driving off, he left the house's occupant very much a sole one.

For a little while, Vincent wondered what he was doing here; shouldn't Gail be with him? He wanted her to come down the stairs, as if she lived here, smiling at his return and hugging him, her kiss promising so much for later. But she had her own home, which he was no longer part of - he wasn't sure if he had ever been - and this was his.

He began tearing open the tops of a few boxes, merely glancing at their contents, hardly noticing what they were. He went up to his bed, it had been surprisingly quick to fit up, and lay there, pulling a curtain back to see the setting sun. There were no flatlands here, no birdcalls, marshes, boats or buoys, just an accidental buddleia, pebble-dashed houses, their green roof pantiles long gone, a newly planted lollipop tree on the pavement which would take years to grow and the inevitable squashed beer cans in the gutter.

He thought of the dead man, he hoped it had been sudden for him. But it was a separate, distant thing, in the past, merely a haphazard collection of random coordinates; an accident. Like history, he said to himself, it was the unintended consequences of men's actions. In the morning, before unpacking much more, he would go to the college.

CHAPTER 15

As the security guards at the entrance - a recent introduction - let him through, his original anger at the puritanical, moral distortion that had led to his being here returned. He went to the third floor and told a secretary that he wished to see the Principal. When told that she wasn't in and wouldn't be in for at least a week, he sarcastically enquired whether the woman who had written the letter was also away. She was. He laughed, shaking his head in quasi-disbelief and went to his staffroom. There was someone sitting at his desk. Pete was there, too.

"'ello mun,' he greeted him then looked briefly at the man sitting at Vincent's desk. 'Tek noer notice mun, he's shadowin' me, summat like that, he wants to be a lecturer. Wha's bin 'appenin'?'

'You don't know?'

'Yeh I do, I 'eard about it. Coom over 'ere.' They walked to a corner of the room. He continued.

'Don't know what you were supposed to have said, but it weren't racist. Christ, this union branch is useless, they'll go through t'motions, and Eric'll be genuine about it, but he'll get nowhere; you know that. I realise it didn't help by me leavin' it, but where do unions coom from anyway? From t' guilds who were more concerned wi' maintainin' differential incomes an' status between skilled artisans an' labourers than any unified opposition to the status quo. You know this, anyway. They're essentially conservative; strikes are just institutionalised agreements between owners an' wearkers, and there's not gonna be a strike for one mun's unfair dismissal, it's not as if it were about a pay rise or summat, is it. 'ave yer seen the Principal?'

'She's away.'

'Convenient. Anyone else?'

'No.'

'Dan's bin lookin' for yer, 'e's in cluss, should be finished soon.'

173

A student of both of them came into the room. 'Hello Vincent,' she smiled then asked Pete if he could spare some time helping her with an essay. He nodded to his colleague and beckoned the girl to sit with him.

Vincent went along the corridor to Dan's usual classroom. He was an elderly psychology lecturer who held a part-time position. As he neared the room a score of students came out, some of them also being taught by Vincent and who greeted him, mostly warmly. He found it difficult to believe that he would probably never see them again, at least inside of a classroom. As the last of them left, he walked over to Dan sitting at his desk who told him to grab a chair. He did, and sat facing him.

Dan, who on occasions had jokingly told their shared pupils that sociology wasn't a proper subject and to 'take no notice of the tall guy,' frowned at him.

'I heard about the sacking. Sorry to be brutal, but I don't think you've got a chance. How d'you feel? Pretty alone, I guess.'

He looked at his listener in silence for a while.

'Look, it doesn't matter what you said, they'll twist it, they can't seem to help themselves, they're full of it, the ideology, the movement - and it *is* a movement - has a grasp on our life, it's become a sort of corruption which appears to be growing exponentially across the Western world.

You know, if you made a case out of this, you wouldn't win; they've probably got it in for you for something else. It seems bloody ironic doesn't it, you who's been teaching scores of Africans for years. God, I'd be pissed off too. Unfortunately, your hatred of it - and I know you feel that - is pretty entrenched also. What about going to the Governors? Are you going to?'

Vincent shook his head. Dan leant towards him.

'The reason you haven't reported it to them is because you feel that they'd be just as liberal and righteous as your coordinator was, they would be on her side. Who *are* they, Vincent? Forgive the rhetorical question, but this is what I think. Alright, I know we've debated before about your subject versus mine, and I know it's not the right place, but think about this when you're on your own. Try to feel it.

They represent your mother don't they; the baby not being recognised, mum changing your nappy when you hadn't shit, giving the breast when you weren't hungry; your barely-born needs unmet.' He paused. 'How did you get on in the staffroom? Shouldn't think they're going to do much. Maybe those in that room are your father taking sides with mum. Think it over at your leisure; it's an awful lot to think about, to accept. It's a lifetime isn't it. You may never recognise it emotionally. I hope you do.'

Vincent deflected what had been said. 'Women think bald men look sexy because their heads look like cocks, don't you think? Plus, it reminds them of a baby, therefore they have both sex and maternity, a double whammy.'

'Stop it Vince, you know what you're doing. You did nothing because you thought that the frail child, yet again, would be taken no notice of, be ignored; unrecognised, be lonelier, more desperate maybe. Yes? This liberalism stuff is very much a presenting case for you, isn't it. Of course it's important, but for you it's a manifestation, a symptom.

I know you're aware of this, that without a value system to internalise we would probably be psychotic and, arguably, everything is, if you like, distorted, because everything's a construct. It's a particular *form* of distortion you hate: the worldview of political correctness, and as minor and laughable as it's made out to be, it represents for you, the child, a denial of what *is*, a disbelief. You hate it because it's saying truth *isn't*, therefore you are *not.'*

He paused. 'Look, I'm sorry about all this, but please think on what I've said. Don't let it be submerged even further by your anger.'

Vincent stood. 'See you, Dan.'

'Any time, remember that.'

He left and returned to the staffroom. He felt lost again. He wanted to get it over with. Eric, the union rep, was the only one there.

'Pete just said he'd seen you. Sorry about what happened.'

'Going to do anything about it?'

His listener looked a little shame-faced.

'Not sure how we can fight it for you if there were no witnesses, it's the coordinator's word against yours. We can try of course, but...'

Vincent went to his desk, he knew there were two large plastic bags in its bottom draw and took them swiftly out and began throwing folders, pens, sheets of paper and books from the other drawers into them. Eric went across to a filing cabinet and silently handed him another bag.

D'you want a hand?'

'No, I can manage.'

'I am sorry about all this, but I will try to get you as much cash as I can. They can make it a redundancy payment or something; shouldn't think they'd want the local press to hear about this. I'll try my damndest to get you a good reference, with your CV I guess you're pretty employable anyway. All the best, mate, we'll have a drink sometime.'

Vincent didn't hear the last sentence; he was struggling down the stairs with his heavy potpourri of pedagogy. Maybe he would think about what Dan had said another time. He went into the car park, got to his car; put his bags in the boot. We're born alone and die alone, he mused as he started it. He felt at this moment that in between times we were alone also.

At the end of the short journey he emptied the boot and placed its contents in his hallway among some other things he hadn't bothered to put in their long-ordained places. Was it all some sort of rather malign fate? He scorned the insipid idea; it was on the level of a football manager saying, after his team had lost, that it wasn't meant to be - a fatalistically determined result meaning his players may as well have sat in the centre circle having a coffee and a smoke and not bothering to touch the ball.

He went to his local cafe and sat wondering whether there was some sort of arbitration available. What, though, if he got a hefty sum from the college? Should he accept it, or return it telling them he had done nothing wrong and would fight for his job? Unthinkingly he jotted a few notes for his next topic, deviancy, before realising there probably wouldn't be a next topic, not at this college, anyway.

The unfairness of it welled up; he threw it off as best he could. Perhaps he should take any money offered, see it as a challenge to move on to another institution, a different atmosphere, different students; he hoped there were Africans. He put his bits of paper away. He imagined the cockney man, if he were still alive, walking into the café. 'Gawd, it's Al cappuccino. Wot you writin'? A note to Don Corleone?'

He looked around him: the photo of the lunching riveters astride a New York girder tilted on the wall, a Cartier-Bresson of the Sacre-Coeur next to it; bright leaves on the graveyard trees of the church opposite seen from under the awning where Vera the waitress sat with yet another cigarette, her smoke blowing across the open door.

He liked to learn a few words from foreign languages, now rapidly becoming local dialects; 'Hello,' 'Please,' and 'Thanks,' which, after a struggle, he'd remembered in Turkish, Polish and Lithuanian, but not in Romanian. On a whim, he scrawled a phonetic of a Romany 'Hello' and held it up. Vera frowned, shook her head and mouthed *Bunaziua.*

Theirs were the only movements inside or outside the shop. Its owner, legs apart, looked at nothing, a customer stared at his cappuccino froth, the local butcher, grey hair thick at the back, rested his chin on a hand, a woman sat in a corner reading. He wanted to harvest it all, bind it, carry it home, place it on a sill in the sun, sit and look at it, every piece of it, slowly, considerately, thinking of nothing else; certainly not of the happenings of the last few days, weeks, months.

Vera put on her coat and passed him as he rose from the table. 'La revedere' she said.

'*Lahreveedaree,* he replied. She shook her head again. He was still struggling.

He saw Gail again a year almost to the day after Billy died. He was waiting outside a station for a group of students who wanted his company in celebrating their passing an Access course he had created at his new college just a mile away. It was at a recently opened African restaurant in Green Street, not far from where the old football stadium was being demolished.

He had, still feeling some anger though a little less consuming because of the money he had, albeit reluctantly, accepted, been attempting to consider Dan's analysis, trying to recognise it, not through his intelligence but letting it grow inside of him, however difficult, perhaps impossible to face. There hadn't been much success so far. He had also been thinking of the things Gail had so angrily thrown at him. He knew, eventually, he needed to consider both their views, reflect on them; make his child *feel* them. Knew he would have to.

She was walking on the opposite side of the road, looking pale, slightly thinner and wearing neat, rather nondescript clothes; but it was still her, the woman he had found, loved, had lived with. She hadn't seen him, he wondered how she would have reacted if she had, or indeed, if she would have responded at all.

He stood there, head turning, watching her, his body almost rooted. He looked at her back then lost sight of her; so many shops, stalls, people. Then he saw her once more, peering into a shop window with a characteristic frown. Then he was looking at the restaurant's flyer he'd been given, and reading intently every word and number on it.

He couldn't escape into this activity for long. The flyer was nudged out of his hand by the elbow of a cyclist as he pedalled past knocking into an elderly woman two metres in front of Vincent. She stumbled and he went forward to steady her as the rider swerved through the packed pavement. It reminded him of the towpath incident. It was difficult to get near him. He shouted at him.

'This is a pavement, it's illegal to cycle on it; in some countries it's called a sidewalk. See the clue there?'

People moved on without turning their heads. 'Cockin' a deaf 'un.' he thought the cockney man would have said. He returned to where he'd been standing thinking of what he would like to do to the rider if he saw him sitting on a saddle again, too lazy to dismount and push. He wanted to take it out on something or someone, let his frustrations out again, despite targets perhaps illogically founded, as Dan might say.

Lumps of his anger came almost separately to the surface as he waited on the pavement. He compiled a mental list: cooks who splattered sauerkraut, olive oil and mayonnaise when told he didn't want dressing, the server surprised, saying, 'It comes that way,' and what could he do about people walking in the street scooping food into their mouths - as the French say, 'Only animals eat standing up' - throw petrol bombs into all the sushi bars and Macdonald's he could find?

And the decorators who tape the glass in window frames because they can't cut in neatly with a brush; would he ever be in a position to sack eighty percent of the country's brush-wielding artisans? Let alone the throwing down, without breaking stride, of beer cans, used food cartons, bits of paper on pavements - was he too harsh in thinking of starting a movement to create a statutory law enforcing the removal of litter louts' hands? He thought of Gail asking him, when he moaned about another wobbly cafe table, whether he intended to ask a barista to lie under the unbalanced leg.

And the bigger ones. Maybe he could try to help change wholesale perceptions somehow. America's apparently growing, manipulated hatred of Muslims, for example, seemingly unaware that it's the majority anti-jihadist, non-fundamentalists that were the potential enemies of Daesh. Could he effectively point out to people that liberalism can no longer export its ideas, its wished-for hegemony of human rights and democracy - whatever these really mean - to the rest of the world? Arguably, the military extension of these has led to the rise of Islamic State, the spread of terrorism, the death of millions and the flood of refugees destabilising Europe.

Perhaps - and closer to his heart - he could help create a consensus that saw the money spent on building ninety-storey egotistic legacies instead of being used to build city streets which celebrate their inhabitants and not celebrate architects, as morally wrong.

And was it possible to make any dents into what was becoming an impenetrable wedge of a neo-fascism that would, eventually, almost literally promulgate the idea that the maximisation of professional career opportunities would perhaps only be achieved if you were a one-eyed Jewish lesbian negress with a limp, thus diluting the idea of a meritocracy even further? No, he couldn't change the world, though he would like a world stage, but wasn't sure he could tread its boards adequately, or even where the theatre was.

But perhaps he should put his money where his political mouth was and actually do something - instantly academicising, he decided that everything was political anyway; it wasn't just about assassinations, coups, elections, but any individual or group that had power or potential power over other individuals; a father telling his teenage daughter to be home by midnight, for example. And wasn't what he'd done, political? To hit back, however ineffectively, against an enforced moral leadership?

He would have to keep it small, individualistic, manageable, he couldn't structure it, just get the justifiable vexation - he grinned at the old-fashioned sound of the word - and anger from his loathing of so many pieces of this planet out of himself.

Referring to the personal, he thought of the surfeit of 'I means' which increasingly began people's sentences, suggesting that any following statement without the preamble of 'I mean' was potentially disingenuous, and which was often followed by 'you know,' placing the onus of articulate explanation onto the listener, and there was … He knew he could do little positive, educate on a large scale, only be more destructive. Another rampage perhaps - maybe he was lucky to get away with the last one, maybe not - the targets specifically chosen, more considered, planned, achievable.

He would have to work out what, how and when. This could be his next project. He would begin it soon. Maybe, just maybe it would be more successful than the last one, his search for a woman. This time it would be a search for some sort of revenge.

His students then came laughing out of the station and he walked with them down the slight hill. Pictures, images, that had been lying still, whirled around, released: Gail putting on her veiled hat for him, the blouse with the shoulder pads that fascinated him, though not quite knowing why, the knotted scarf around her head when he'd first seen her and, again, singing 'Bye Bye Blackbird.'

He walked along, his companions hopping into the kerb and back again to give themselves room in the crowd, smelt the sharp sweetness of chips and vinegar and the musky cloud of cheap corn oil. He felt for a nanosecond the prick of a tear, then the detachment, the intellectualising, chopping into him like the rigid hands of a masseur on the back of a client.

Silently naming the type faces on the shop fascias, he observed, as ever, the unnecessary apostrophes, the PVC windows aesthetically corrupting Edwardian houses in a side street, and noticed some police blocking part of the main road while builders lorries were moving on to the stadium site. There was a blue and white striped tape. He thought, wanting to laugh hysterically, that it said 'Polite notice' and 'Do not be cross.'